INSIDE MADELEINE

ALSO BY PAULA BOMER

Nine Months

INSIDE MADELEINE

paula bomer

"Eye Socket Girls" first appeared in *Girls: An Anthology* (Global City Press), "Breasts" first appeared in Everyday Genius, "Reading to the Blind Girl" first appeared in *Storyglossia*, "Down the Alley" first appeared in *New York Tyrant*, "Cleveland Circle House" first appeared in *Fiction*, "Pussies" first appeared in *Night Train*, "Two Years" first appeared in Nerve, "Inside Madeleine" first appeared in *The Literary Review*

Published by
Soho Press, Inc.
853 Broadway
New York, NY 10003

Library of Congress Cataloging-in-Publication Data

Bomer, Paula.
[Short stories. Selections]
Inside Madeleine / Paula Bomer.
p. cm
ISBN 978-1-61695-309-6
eISBN 978-1-61695-310-2
1. Short stories. I. Title.
PS3602.O653I67 2014
813'.6—dc23   2013045386

Interior design by Janine Agro, Soho Press, Inc.

Printed in the United States of America

10 9 8 7 6 5 4 3 2 1

For my mother

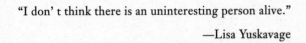

"I don' t think there is an uninteresting person alive."

—Lisa Yuskavage

table of contents

• eye socket girls •

I DON'T WANT TO JUMP OUT ANY WINDOW. I just want to breathe something that makes me feel like living. They pump the air in here out of machines. It stinks like Play-Doh. Open a window, please—I won't jump—I'm not a suicide patient. I just don't eat.

My neighbors don't eat either. Eye socket girls. Nurses drag them with their IVs to the scale. Some girls get weighed once a day, others, two or three times. Liquids pump into our bodies through plastic tubing, adding pounds to our emaciated frames. We don't like the pounds. We look voraciously at one another. We envy the protruding bones of someone who is that much closer to not being here at all.

You may think that I don't know I'm emaciated. I know every curve and angle of my rib cage. I know my breasts have disappeared completely and my nipples lay flat against my chest. I am aware that the new girl has hair growing out of her face. This girl's body sprouts hair like moss on a tree stump, everywhere, to keep itself warm, to protect itself.

I know about these things. I'm aware of the effects of my disease.

It started with sesame seeds, one by one. I rolled each one between my forefinger and thumb, and then I placed it on my tongue. Salt and oil. Nuttiness. I counted each one. I counted how long I rolled each seed greasily between my fingers. Ten seconds to roll. Ten seconds in the mouth. I ate seventy-four seeds that day. It became my thing. My personal toy. I counted sesame seeds for the rest of the year.

Now this hospital is exerting itself on me. It's like a muscleman on top of me. It's attempting to take away my grip on life. I count the seconds and minutes from when I wake up to when the nurse does her rounds in the morning. I count the seconds and minutes I visit with Dr. Johansen every Saturday morning. I count the seconds and minutes it takes me to eat my meals.

Yesterday they brought in the new girl. The one I mentioned. She looks young, maybe sixteen, but it's hard to tell. Where's she been hiding I wonder? She's so wasted away she can't really stand up. Her skin is blue-green, veins throbbing, screaming for oxygen. They pushed her by me in a wheelchair, a hospital gown draped over her, an oxygen tank rolling along side of her. She is the Master of all Masters. Down boy, she says to her screaming veins, down! I'll let you know when you can eat.

She has a tiny bit of blond hair on her head. I bet at one time it was thick and shiny, falling in cascades down her back. Now it falls out in handfuls. Bald patches on her scalp. Her face and arms are furry, though, with dark, fine hair.

They haven't made her get up and go to the scale this morning. They just keep her in bed, IVs galore floating life back into her body. Poor thing, she's too wasted to protest. But once she regains some strength, I bet she'll be a contender. She seems blessed with stamina. I never made it that far. Not yet at least. I count how often they check on her and for how long. They've checked her three times this morning, at half hour intervals.

Here in the ward, we outnumber them. They may walk around with charts and fancy white outfits, but we're all starving to death. Sure, the IVs fatten us up for a while, but then we go home. Then we resume life as we know it. Life as a battle of will. And we're winners.

That's why people fight us. No one likes to see a young girl win. We're supposed to be nice, well-behaved things. Pliable, fearful things that cry a lot, especially when we have our periods. I don't get my period anymore. I haven't bled since I was fourteen.

It happens in high school. Other girls start losing all their power—other girls start only caring about boys—they get fat and self-conscious, their grades slip. They hang out with each other, stuffing their faces with Twinkies and chips. They lie around, watching movies, saying oohh, I wish I was Winona Ryder. She's so skinny.

They become shy and don't talk much in class. When a teacher calls on them, they giggle and don't know the answer. They're too busy dreaming about being a movie star. Dreaming about an ass they'll never have.

Not me. I've never lost power. In high school, I got straight A's. I ran on the cross-country track team. I had the lead in every play, I ran the student council, I tutored the learning disabled, I did everything and then some. At home, I came in when I wanted, I bought all the clothes I wanted, I wore all the make-up I wanted.

And I fucked any guy that I wanted. I fucked the quarterback, the editor of the school paper, and the richest guy in the entire school. I count every bite of every thing I eat. I had a notebook for a while, where I wrote it all down. Half an apple. Two bites of toast. What can I say? Self-control doesn't begin to describe my power.

Oh, here they come again to go check on the new girl. Cute thing.

All the nurses have sober, professional expressions. The doctor's in a hurry. The bitchier the face they make, the worse off the girl is. They're close to smiling when they come by my bed. I'm fit as fiddle. I'm nearing release day. This girl—they all have post-enema expressions when they return from visiting her. I know what they're thinking. They think, she has everything in the world and she starves herself like a third-world victim. She has gold jewelry and a dad on the stock market and this is her thanks. Fool, they think. She deserves to die.

As soon as she gets better, I'll befriend her. As soon as she starts getting weighed regularly, they'll have to pull her and her IV along, right past my bed. We all look at each other here. She'll notice me. She'll notice my age. I'm twenty, but

I look older. She'll look at me and see herself in me. She'll think, am I going to look like that ten years from now? Curiosity will get to her.

I wonder what her name is? The nurses won't tell me. I ask them, I say, hey nurse, what's the new girl's name? I say, hey she's cute. They sneer at me. But I know it. Yeah, I don't need their help. It's something pretty. A flowery name like Melissa or Allison. Something WASPy and clean. Let's call her Melissa. Melissa oh Melissa.

I walk to her bed. She's still weak and I'm as thick as a horse. It's late, maybe two in the morning. She's awake, waiting for me. Her eyes shine in the dark like doe eyes, wide and wet, her pupils dilated. I sit next to her on the bed because there's lots of room. We talk late into the night. I tell her she's beautiful. She confesses to having taken handfuls of laxatives, day in and day out, without eating a thing. I slip my hand under the covers. Her hand comes crawling up to mine, quick and bony, like a beetle. I grab it—hold onto her dry, scaly hand. And that's it. We just hold hands for a while. That's all.

You see, everyone has her story. She confesses it to you, crying like a spanked child, mouth all distorted like a baby's. Her eyes sear you when they look at you, nestled eyes in the skeleton of her face. Her eyes plead for more punishment, more discipline. We're all dying for the whip, each and every one of us. We crave it.

I look at the clock. Here come the doctors, off to visit my Melissa. I count each second they stay with her. *Cheer up*, I want to yell at them as they walk by. They're walking by rather quickly now, scowling. What are they in such a hurry for? Here they come back again, off to fetch some fancy equipment it seems. What is this girl up to, I wonder? Does she bite them when they try to touch her?

Oh Melissa, you're mad, I know, but you're beautiful. You need me. Ignore the doctors. Push away those nurses. Let me be your one. Let me touch your heart, straining your cavernous chest. Let me push down on it with my fists, let me push your heart out, let me push. Here they come with her. Wheeling her past me. So fast. The whole floor's buzzing.

They can't save her.

But I can.

• breasts •

LOLA SPENCER HAD THE SORT OF BREASTS THAT DEFINE A WOMAN. They were gorgeous perfect things, pink-nippled, sized like cantaloupes, firm and white. They were big and she was small. The rest of her existed to accentuate her breasts; her hips were narrow, her waist a tiny circle, her little pale legs ended in child's feet. Her head was small and heart shaped, her features pale and slightly receding. Indeed, it was as if every other part of her got out of the way to make way for her breasts. Yes, Lola's breasts were the sort of breasts that made a girl feel special, feel as if she were not destined for an ordinary life. When she was sixteen, she dropped out of high school and took a bus from Detroit to New York City.

It was 1986, and it was the end of June. New York was a shithole; the filthy stench of summer had begun to descend. When Lola got off the bus at Port Authority, she grabbed her duffel bag and the fake white patent leather clutch purse that she'd held primly in her lap the whole ride, and with these two worldly possessions, she snaked her way through the dark tunnels until she managed to take an escalator up to the street. The sun slapped her face with a hot hand, and the air was rich with the fumes of urine and car exhaust. She blinked and froze. Large people, loud people, people towering over the tiny Lola, were walking and running and standing and screaming and going in every direction. Blindly, she marched forward. She had the address for a YWCA, but she also had other ideas. Vague ideas, but ideas nonetheless.

She had five hundred dollars in her white clutch purse. She'd made the money rather quickly, working the drive-through at a McDonald's in Detroit, where her enormous chest strained against the polyester shirt of her uniform. Occasionally, she popped a button, and the white lace of her cheap bra would sneak out. There had been an older gentleman who came every morning for an Egg McMuffin. He drove a beige Cadillac, and when his window rolled down with the touch of a button, the smell of leather and cologne wafted up to Lola. It was the best smell Lola had ever smelled. It smelled of money, but of something else, too. He thanked her solemnly and gave her a dollar tip. And in those two words, "thank you," and in his dark eyes and dark skin and hair, she sniffed something very exotic, very foreign. The dollar tip turned to five and soon enough, she couldn't wait to hear his voice in the telecom, asking gruffly for an Egg McMuffin. She'd unbutton her uniform just a little, and she'd wet her thin little lips. The months went on and at Christmas, he said his thank you, his voice thick with appreciation, and gave her two one hundred dollar bills. She never saw him again, but by the end of June, yes, she had five hundred dollars in her purse and was on her way.

As luck would have it, Lola's little feet took her downtown. Encased in tight, strappy sandals with four-inch heels, her infantile toenails were painted a cherry red. She marched and marched. A man stopped and watched her walk by. A few blocks later, another man yelled something in Spanish at her. Lola, a brave soldier, went onward. A few blocks later, an overweight man sitting on a beach chair in his doorway said, "Nice tits." Yes, she was special. She'd been special in Detroit, at her high school. The looks, the lewd comments, the occasional grabbing. But what good was that, being special at John Adams High School in Detroit? She was in New York City. She'd come to the right place.

Her feet began to die on her. The endless stretch of asphalt darkened and cooled off ever so slightly. She marched forward, more slowly now, but there was blood on her feet and her arm ached from carrying her duffel. How long had she been walking? At one point, she turned left, and she found herself surrounded by the sort of people by whom she always imagined she should be surrounded. Skinny guys with spikey hair and bad pockmarks, weighed down by the metal in their belts. Girls with breasts like hers, tightly encased in tank tops, their dyed red hair the color of a sunset. The make-up! The cigarettes! She was in the East Village, but she didn't know that yet. What she did know was she was going to cry if she had to keep walking and cry she did not want to do. No, not

Lola. She was tough. She wasn't going to cry just because her feet were bleeding.

On the corner of First Street and Second Avenue was a cinder block building with a sign that said Mars Bar. It was a crappy little bar with nary a beer sign in the grimy windows. Lola liked it immediately; she liked small things, being small herself—well, for the most part. She went in and sat on a barstool, dropping her duffel bag to the dirty ground, her white clutch in her hands.

"What can I getcha?" said a muscular, black-haired girl.

"I'll have a peppermint schnapps, please." This had often been the drink of choice in the backseat of a Camaro, cruising the strip in Detroit.

The girl raised her eyebrow. Lola noticed it was very thick, thick as a cigar.

"How 'bout a bourbon?" Then she leaned forward and whispered, "I'm helping you out here. You can't drink peppermint schnapps."

Lola sat up a little straighter. "A bourbon then."

It was a welcome burn and Lola quickly had two more. Her feet were feeling better already. Men came into the bar. Women, too. Occasionally, Lola waved at someone who looked interesting, but nothing seemed to happen as she thought it would. Four bourbons later, the bartender took her upstairs to where she lived and laid her out on her futon couch. Lola had never seen a futon. She immediately threw up, but the bartender handled it well.

The next morning, Rebecca, the bartender, made some tea and toast.

"Where you from?"

"Detroit. Thanks for the tea."

"You can stay here until you find a place."

Lola sat up. "You know, I'm not hungover."

"Great." Rebecca got down on the floor and started doing sit-ups. "But if you keep waving hello to strangers like you did last night, you'll be dead before you're ever hungover."

"Strangers are all I have here. You're a stranger."

"You're not in Kansas anymore, Lola."

"Detroit ain't in Kansas."

"You know what I mean."

Lola thought for a minute. "No, I don't."

Rebecca was silent, finishing her sit-ups. When she did get up she went to Lola on the futon and held her face gently in her hands. "You don't know what I mean, do you?"

"That's right. I don't know what you mean."

Rebecca kissed her gently and Lola felt a fluttering. She'd had a boyfriend briefly in high school, but nothing much happened with him, so she got rid of him. This felt different. Rebecca picked up Lola's swollen, blood-stained feet and began to lick them. This went on for a surprisingly long time, until Lola began to get very, very sleepy. Then, carefully, so as not to disturb Lola, Rebecca removed Lola's shirt and pulled down her bra, leaving it hanging there awkwardly, around the bottom of her breasts. "Damn," Rebecca said, and then she was lost in them. Lola, stretched out on the futon, flung her arms over her head, and let the fluttering feeling go on.

Lola worked Monday, Tuesday, and Wednesday nights, and Rebecca worked the rest. It had been easy to get the other bartender fired; he was rude, stole from the register, and drank a bottle of vodka a night. All Rebecca had to do was tell the owner the truth.

The first thing Lola did was buy a pair of sneakers, but still she didn't match the East Village hipsters in their high tops. She just looked like a five year old with huge breasts, so she found a pair of boots with a nice sized heel on them and that did the trick.

Mondays and Tuesdays she made around a hundred dollars. Wednesdays weren't much better. That first day she walked from Port Authority, when she felt she'd brought her breasts to the right place, had faded to a quaint memory in little over a month's time. She was glad to be where she was, but she was surprised she wasn't getting bigger tips, better offers. Men had looked, men gave her money, one even offered her a job to dance naked at a dive in Tribeca. But nothing felt right. Nothing had felt right since the day Rebecca took her in, and she was getting restless. Lola appreciated Rebecca, very much. But she knew it wasn't forever.

Four weeks into the job and it was heading toward August, the July warmth giving way to a numbing, stifling hotness and filth that was, well, August in the East Village. Mars Bar had no air conditioner, and the two fans in the window whirred, loudly blowing hot air everywhere. Lola tied her pale hair back in a ponytail; otherwise, it whipped around and stuck to her moist face. Teardrops of sweat dripped into her cleavage. It was Wednesday, and the beginning of her shift, but her mind was already on the night being over. She'd have four days off to read magazines and shop. She'd clean up the apartment, too, which Rebecca liked her to do.

"What do you have on draft?" a man said, and Lola stood up right away, as if she were in the military and he'd just barked an order.

He sat and drank and looked at her breasts.

"Wipe that lipstick off your face."

Lola took a white bar napkin from the neat pile she'd just made and rubbed at her mouth.

His name was Christopher. He was six feet three, skinny, face and arms hairless, with large, smooth hands. He had a crew cut of black hair and black eyes and a tattoo of a dragon on one forearm and the name MARCY on the other. His father was in jail, which he was annoyed about. He had a motorcycle and he smoked filterless Pall Malls. He took her home that night and it hurt, but it was the right thing to do. She woke up the next morning in an apartment very much like the one she shared with Rebecca, and only a few blocks away, but she knew her life had changed forever.

He left that day, without saying where he was going. She got to work cleaning. There wasn't much to clean. When he got back around four in the afternoon, he did it to her again, and this time it felt good. Not as good as Rebecca, but it didn't matter. She was his now, and that's the way she wanted it.

Lola sat next to him on the couch where they both held bowls of canned raviolis on their laps, and she let her knees gently touch his.

"We're going to rob that bar you work at. Tonight."

The only thing Lola could think to say was, "Rebecca's working tonight."

"Who fucking cares? You got the keys, right?"

"No."

"Well then we'll have to do it before she closes."

They drank on Avenue B, not far from Mars Bar. Occasionally, he leaned into her and she thought that he smelled a lot like that man in the Cadillac. Where was he now? Pulling into his driveway in Grosse Pointe, or some other posh Detroit suburb? Going home to a family? A wife who loved him? College-age children with futures? The music in the bar was loud and someone was singing, "Yeah, yeah it's alright, yeah-ah, it's alright. Baby, it's alright, oh oh, baby it's alright." The bar they were in had air conditioning, which felt delicious to Lola, and she could feel a thin film of salt dry on her skin. Her nipples hardened up into little stiff puckers, and she leaned against the bar and arched her back a bit. Yes, Christopher had that smell, the smell of a man, a real man, the smell of something exotic, someone foreign. He'd told her he was part Cherokee and that was why he was hairless. It was destiny she told herself, it was out of her control, just like the size of her breasts.

It was nearing four in the morning and all the bars were closing. It was only three blocks away. Three blocks and everything would change. She'd have that future she always dreamed about, though vaguely.

"Hurry up."

Lola skipped along behind him, trying to catch up with his long strides. She was wearing her boots and it still wasn't easy catching up. But she liked the view from behind, yes. His filthy black jeans, the nunchucks sticking brazenly out of his back pocket. The way he stooped over. Did he have a gun? She doubted it. It was all about his hands, his large, hairless hands.

As they got near Mars Bar, a seemingly homeless man with white spittle around the corners of his mouth, the stench of rot wafting forth from his body and a tiny little crack vial in his hand, tried to stop Christopher.

"Man, man, can you spare some change. I'm hungry, man . . ."

Christopher hit the man, and Lola watched him fall to the sidewalk.

They were seconds from the bar. The lights were out. For a moment, it was as if New York had gone dark, and the only thing glowing were the man's eyes, staring up at her from where he lay injured on the sidewalk.

"Help me," he said, and Lola stopped for a moment before a crashing noise jarred her attention away.

It was Rebecca pulling the gate down, the metal scraping

loudly as the gate fell to the sidewalk. But she hadn't locked it yet, no, not yet. Christopher was a bit ahead now; she scurried to catch up. She saw the nunchucks come out of his pocket and for a moment, she wasn't the woman she thought she was. She was afraid. She looked away, in fact, she looked down, and she saw that she, too, was glowing, not just that poor man's eyes, no, but her pale breasts were glowing, and with a little effort she could hide her face in that whiteness, with just a little effort, she could close herself up in all her luck, in all that beauty.

• reading to the blind girl •

Maggie immediately loved Anya Lander, her anthropology professor at Boston University, like many students did. This was the first most important thing that happened to her at college. It was, in a way, her first chance in life. She wanted to please Anya. And she was an excellent student, but recently she'd fallen in love.

She was in love with Tony. He was ten years older than her and in a band that was going to be signed, she just knew it. Tony gave her hope, at least some of the time. And so did Anya. Anya radiated hope, as well as energy and enthusiasm and possibility. And Maggie craved hope. Her parents had died when she was seven. And her uncle and his wife, who raised her, never meant much to her. When she got the scholarship to BU, she left Indiana in a hurry.

The second week of the introductory course—which was a huge lecture with about ninety students—Anya Lander asked if anyone could volunteer to read to Caroline, a sight-impaired student enrolled in the class. The materials being used were not available in Braille. Anya (as she asked her students to call her) stood at the front of the class, looking out at the vast room of people, her long, curly, truly wild hair loose around her shoulders, a brown denim mini skirt revealing her long, shapely legs. And Maggie, sitting at the back of the class like always, felt her hand rise. Maggie could see the entirety of the students in front of her—no one else raised a hand.

"Great. We have a volunteer," Anya said, smiling fetchingly. "Come up after class and see me," she said to Maggie, her large blue eyes shining all the way to the back of the class. Maggie's heart started to race. It stayed that way for the rest of the hour, thumping away, making her breathe with difficulty. She didn't know why she'd volunteered. It had nothing to do with wanting to help a blind girl. Maggie wasn't really that sort. Her immediate, yearning feelings for Anya were what propelled her.

When the class ended, Maggie numbly walked up to Anya Lander. Close up, Anya had acne scars, and her head seemed large for her body, but she was still a supremely magnetic person. Standing so close to Anya made Maggie dizzy. And now, here she was. She could practically smell her. One other person remained in the classroom and that was Caroline, the blind girl. She remained seated in the front row, a mousy girl—short, pale skin, unseeing blue eyes, dishwater brown hair unattractively shaped around her face. Her shirt was ill-fitting; in fact, it may have been put on wrongly.

"Thanks so much for volunteering to read to Caroline. What's your name?"

"Maggie. Maggie Drescher."

"Maggie, this is Caroline."

Caroline stuck a hand eagerly in the direction of Maggie. Her other hand gripped a cane. "Nice to meet you. When can we start? I'd like to set up a once a week meeting. Let's find out how our schedules work out and set something up. I'm very anxious to stay with the class. I don't like getting behind in my schoolwork. Can you walk me back to my dorm room? We could figure out everything on the way there." Caroline's fingers closed on Maggie's arm like talons. Anya Lander beamed at Maggie as she guided her new acquaintance out the door.

Caroline was very bossy during the walk, ordering her in a clipped, nervous way. "Turn here. Now go straight."

Caroline's grip was too hard. Later there'd be small, purple bruises on Maggie's arm. Maggie said, "Why don't you just tell me where you live and I'll just walk us there?"

"No. No, that won't do at all in this case, but for other things, that would be great. But for now, I need to always go the same route. I need to learn my way to every class because I can't rely on people taking me around. I'm often by myself."

"Alright," Maggie said.

"Just getting to class is a big ordeal for me," said Caroline, breathing an acrid, nervous breath at Maggie. "I'll get the hang of it by the end of the semester. And then, of course, everything will change again," Caroline snorted, and then barked sharply, "Now take a right!"

When they arrived at Caroline's dorm room, a couple

disentangled themselves from each other and sat up from the bed where they'd been clearly fooling around. "You could knock you know," said the young woman, a chubby, dark-haired girl. The room smelled sweaty.

"You could go to his room for a change," snapped Caroline. "This is Maggie. Maggie, this is my roommate, Shelley, and I assume her boyfriend, Michael."

The couple said meek, watery hellos. Maggie couldn't help but notice Michael's erection pushing against his khakis. After she looked at it, she looked up at him and then at Shelley. They held her gaze.

"Maggie's going to be reading to me for anthropology class, since none of the material is in Braille," Caroline said. "I'll need time alone here with her. We're working out a schedule now. And once I give it to you, you'll have to hump each other somewhere else during our meeting times. Got that?"

They ended up meeting once a week, at one in the afternoon, the day before the anthropology class met. Maggie'd knock on Caroline's door, and Caroline would open the door for her—it took her longer to get to it than it would a seeing person. To her dismay, this bothered Maggie. She felt impatience rise in her as she listened for Caroline's noisy approach. "Hi, come in, come in." Maggie watched her walk toward the bed with its cheap, blue comforter and flowered pillowcases.

Maggie always sat on the floor below Caroline's bed, on a thin, dusty white rug. She stayed an hour or sometimes more.

As the semester progressed, it was often more. The small dorm room, crowded with two twin beds and two desks and two dressers, smelled bad. Often, Maggie would ask if she could open the window to air out the place a bit. Why did it smell? Was it just the smell of other people, a foreign body smell? Maggie's boyfriend Tony smelled. He smelled like sweat and Speedstick deodorant and leather and like cigarettes, even though he didn't smoke, because he spent so much time in bars. Maggie loved his smell. To her, it was life.

Maggie read to her from the carefully chosen Xeroxes: "In many narratives of human evolution there is a similar sense that man may be doomed, that although civilization evolved as a means of protecting man from nature, it is now his greatest threat."

"Huh," snorted Caroline. "I would've been dead meat back then. Left behind for the hyenas to eat. Thank God for civilization and its constructs."

"I don't know if I believe that," said Maggie.

"You better believe it. The blind and the crippled, the retarded and the children and the old people—we're not the fittest. The survival of the fittest, Maggie. Don't forget."

"I bet early man took care of his loved ones."

"Pass that one by Anya. I bet she'd disagree."

"Anya never disagrees with anyone. She lets everyone speak their mind. And then she just looks at you thoughtfully. Sometimes I don't think she believes any of the evolutionary theories."

"I know what you mean," said Caroline. "So why does she teach this stuff?"

"I don't know exactly. Maybe she's such a great teacher because she doesn't believe any of it."

"She's beautiful, isn't she?"

"Anya? Yeah, I guess so. Although she has acne scars. It makes her somewhat vulnerable. It makes her more human."

"Are you beautiful, Maggie?"

There was something nasal in the tone of Caroline's question; a mocking hostility.

"I don't know. I don't think so."

"What do you look like?" Caroline asked. "Tell me," she said, in her demanding, aggressive way.

"Well, I'm tall. I'm five eight. And I'm blonde and I have green eyes."

"You're not fat, that I know from touching you," Caroline said, smugly. "I bet you're beautiful. Yeah."

Maggie felt ashamed. She felt her cheeks get hot.

"I've been told I'm not ugly. That I'm attractive." Caroline put her hands to her face. Maggie looked up at her, this tiny unseeing person scrunched up against the flowered pillows of her bed. She couldn't be more than five feet tall. She was pasty, as if she never was in direct sunlight. Her hair looked dirty. But she had a button nose and her eyes were a striking clear blue. She had large breasts pushing against her oxford button down shirt. She was not ugly, no. "I had a boyfriend at my old school, at my high school. I went to a high school for the blind. He told me I was beautiful. But he was blind. My mother always told me I was beautiful. But that's what mothers tell their kids, no matter what. Not that I know what beautiful is, really, to people like you."

"Where's your boyfriend now?"

"We broke up. He started fucking someone else. A seeing girl. Can you believe it? He was very ambitious."

"Oh, I'm sorry."

"Screw him anyway. She was a snarky bitch. I knew her. She taught at our school. He gets what he deserves. Do you have a boyfriend?"

"I do," said Maggie. "But we fight a lot. We break up a lot. But, yes, I do."

"What does he look like? Is he handsome?"

"I don't know if I would call him handsome. He's not very tall and his hair is thinning. But I think he's the most beautiful person in the world. I can't stop looking at him. I see him in my mind all the time. I guess that's what love does. It makes the way people look unimportant. It blinds you, sort of."

"Nothing blinds you but being blind, Maggie. You'll never know what it means to be blind."

"Of course not! I didn't mean that."

"Well, I guess if I can fantasize what it's like to see, you can pretend to be blind. What the hell. Keep reading."

"Alright. I'm going to start reading from a new piece, okay?"

"Whatever. You're the one who can see."

. . .

That night, Tony and Maggie ordered a pizza and watched a movie in his apartment. His roommate, a guitar player in another band, was out. They had the place to themselves. After the movie, in the near darkness of his room, on his futon, they made love. Maggie tried not to look. She tried to keep her eyes closed, but she couldn't. She didn't like it that way. She opened her eyes and saw his pale skin glowing in the dark. His black hair blending into the night, but separate all the same. He entered her and she gasped. His eyes were like a night beast's, black and shining at her. She didn't stop looking into them until she came, and then she couldn't see at all.

Caroline listened at first, but as the weeks wore on, she mostly wanted to talk. Maggie felt rushed—she read quickly. Often, Caroline interrupted her. Maggie worried that she wasn't doing her job properly—she worried what Anya would think. But Caroline was very aggressive. Very needy. She hated her roommates and wanted to talk about them all the time.

"They think I don't know because I can't see. So they fuck in front of me. I can hear it. The rustling of their clothes. The moist sound of their bodies against each other. I can smell it. I hate them."

"Have you tried talking to them? Telling them it's not okay to do that?"

Caroline's unseeing eyes seemed to try and focus on Maggie. Funny, thought Maggie, this girl has been blind her whole life, but her face, her eyes, still appear to try to see. Caroline looked down from her perch on her bed, and it was her nose that really pointed toward Maggie. Her white oxford shirt was buttoned incorrectly and wasn't very white at all; it was a grayish yellow. Maggie wondered if she should say something to her. She would say that to a friend, she would tell a friend, your shirt's buttoned incorrectly. But with Caroline, she hesitated. She felt the rules were different. And besides, she didn't feel like Caroline was a friend.

"Of course I talk to them about it! I start yelling at them to stop! I'm not one to keep things bottled up inside, surely you've figured that out by now. You know what they do? They laugh. They laugh and keep doing it."

"Maybe you should try and get a new room."

"I don't think so. That's the last thing I need, to try to re-orient myself. They are the ones who should go. They should go straight to hell. Fucking cunts, both of them. Michael's nothing special is he? I mean, I can tell from the way he talks. Once, he let me feel his face, too. I'm right, don't you think? Nothing special, either of them. And Shelley's fat! That I know!"

Maggie decided she hated Caroline's roommates, too. One week, upon arriving to Caroline's room, the two of them were there. Caroline wasn't.

"Oh, Caroline's friend," said Shelley sarcastically, lounging back on the bed with Michael. It was the middle of the day, but clearly they'd been fucking. Maggie was like that with Tony. She wanted to fuck him no matter what time of day, no matter where, no matter anything. She was like them, she thought, her face growing warm.

"You know, Caroline's really upset with your behavior."

"Caroline's really upset about everything," shot back Shelley.

"Stop fucking when she's in the room. She knows. She doesn't like it. It's cruel."

"We don't fuck when she's in the room, not that it's any of your business."

"Somehow, I don't believe you," Maggie said, although her resolve was faltering. Maybe they didn't fuck in front of Caroline. After all, Caroline couldn't see, she couldn't really know.

"Well, believe it. Caroline's an angry bitch. I can't wait until this year's over. I can't wait to live with someone who knows how to properly wash their own damn laundry." Shelley's face was red. She was standing now. "You try living with her. She's impossible. She's dirty, she's mean. She doesn't know how to properly wipe her ass and everything smells like shit in here. She's always fucking angry. You try it. Oh, and she's not here today. She went home. Her mother came to get her. She won't be back until next week."

The semester was coming to an end. Tony broke up with Maggie, this time it seemed for good, although it wasn't and it wouldn't be for another year or so, not until many more break-ups happened would it be for good. Maggie's grades dropped. Most of her professors didn't notice, but Anya did. At the year-end conference, Anya asked Maggie, "What's going on,

Maggie? You haven't handed in your last paper. And the last in-class exam of yours was a bit of a disappointment. As you know, I gave you an A because there was nothing wrong with your exam, but it lacked that special brilliance you always deliver. You have such a gift, Maggie, do you know that? I hate to think you would squander it." She looked at Maggie quizzically, but with some disappointment, some sternness. "A gift like yours is only something if you use it, otherwise you may as well not have it, and sadly, you can't just give it to someone else, can you? Is reading to Caroline interfering with your work in any way? I wanted to ask how that was going. I think it's so wonderful that you're doing it." Anya sat behind her desk, her elbows jutting out neatly, her slim, beautiful hands laying delicately on top of each other, the frizzy strands of her hair sparkling around her head. Suddenly, the late spring's sun flowed in through a window behind the desk and flooded the room with warmth. Maggie flushed. Anya was looking straight at her, with concern. With a detached, professional concern, but with genuine concern.

"My boyfriend broke up with me," Maggie sobbed, much to her shame. She put her head in her hands and cried noisily and wetly. How could it be? How could he not love her like she loved him? He told her, you'll still be beautiful in your thirties. In your forties. You'll be my beautiful wife. He had told her, his dick inside of her, still warm, we'll have children together. Laying on top of her, his thin, small body barely covering her own, his head hanging down next to her ear, we'll have six children. And grandchildren. He pulled out of her and it hurt. Not physically, but it hurt, left her empty. She wanted him inside her always. He stood, naked and so white before her, his black, Italian eyes staring straight into her. And she'd believed him. And she'd never, ever felt so loved, not even as a child. He loved her, in that moment. In that moment, he loved her for the rest of her life. And the next day, he wouldn't return her phone call. Or the next. Or the next.

What more could he want, if she gave him everything? She let him fuck her in the ass. She let him have everything she had. She had ripped open her chest and delivered him her red, bleeding, pumping heart. And now, there was nothing left of her.

"Sorry about last week," Caroline said the following week, upon Maggie's arrival. "I should have called you. My mom had some time off and surprised me by coming down."

"That's alright."

"I'm miserable to be back. I have to get rid of Shelley. She's the goddamn devil. But the year is ending soon. I guess I should just wait it out. Do you have any roommates?"

"Yeah."

"Do you like them?

"No, not really. But we all pay the rent on time. And we have a nice apartment for very little money so I can't imagine any of us ever giving that up. But no, I don't like them. They're very spoiled."

Caroline smiled, looking off into the center of the room. "I'm spoiled. My mother spoils me. She always did everything she could for me. She gave me everything I needed. She'd go to the end of the earth for me."

"Yeah, but . . ."

"But I'm blind?"

Maggie was quiet for a moment. She hated when Caroline finished her sentences, like she had some kind of sixth sense. She'd hate living with Caroline, too, if that's what Caroline was looking for. Suddenly, Maggie was scared. What if Caroline wanted to live with her? Never, thought Maggie, to her shame.

"Just yesterday, Shelley came in and I knew Michael was with her. I said hi to both of them and Shelley said, Michael's not here. I said, yes he is. I heard four footsteps come in. Then they start fooling around. I can hear the slight rustling, you know? I can smell the mustiness of her cunt. So I start toward them. I was just so angry, you know. I wanted to pull them apart, rip them apart. And Shelley's laughing, moving so quickly—Michael, too—that I can't grab them. The whole time I was yelling, I know you're here! I know what you are doing! And I was falling over the furniture, trying to grab them. They just laughed at me. And then they ran out."

"That is so awful, Caroline."

"Why would they do that?"

"I don't know. I really don't know."

"Do your roommates do shit like that to you?"

"Well, not like that." Maggie thought for a moment. "I have

two roommates. I don't really like them. But we're not that nasty to each other, either. Listen, Caroline, I better start reading. It's getting late." She felt bad saying it. But it was true.

She read: "Although we usually fail to think of it in this way, the world around us today is just one of countless possible worlds. The millions of species of plants, animals, and insects we see around us are the expression of myriad interacting processes, including chance—perhaps especially chance. At any point in its prehistory, a species might just as easily have taken a different direction, given a slightly altered confluence of events, thus leaving today's world a slightly different place."

A year later, on a particularly freezing, windy day in March, Maggie was walking down Commonwealth Avenue toward a class that she didn't really care about. She hadn't mustered up the emotion to care about anthropology, or anything really, in quite some time at that point. Even Anya Lander held no power for Maggie. Anya! Who once meant so much to her. Who cared for her and seemed to lead the way for Maggie when she was a new student, a new person in Boston. Maggie saw Anya in class, a seminar on the history of science, but that was it. The wind blew viciously, cruelly, as if full of hate. Maggie wore red high heel boots and jeans and a short motorcycle jacket, the jacket that once belonged to Tony. Her head was uncovered and her thin, blonde hair whipped in the wind. She was shivering large, spastic shivers, her hands shoved deep in the cold animal hide of her coat. She was deeply hungover.

She'd taken to getting very drunk and having sex with just about anybody, as many nights as she could.

Caroline came walking toward her, alone, tap tapping her cane, her face purple-red with the cold, and perhaps fear. Her coat was buttoned wrongly, as her shirts often were when Maggie read to her, now a year ago. They had not been in touch since then, even though Maggie had promised to stay in touch, to call or write letters that Caroline's mother would then read to her. The wind blew fiercely and Caroline hovered, as if she were about to fall. It had been so long since Maggie had seen her. Maggie dug her chin down into her neck to brace herself against the wind, but it didn't help. Nothing did.

This was her chance. As the two young women approached each other, a great gust of wind sang in Maggie's ridiculously uncovered, raw ears. It was a searing noise, high-pitched and unearthly, like a band of desperate angels screeching to be heard. The noise penetrated the cold, superceded it, and gave Maggie a sharp, abrupt headache.

They were both alone, walking toward each other, in opposite directions. This was her chance to help a blind girl through an impossible day, through one moment of a horrible, horrible day. Or, Maggie could walk right by her, and Caroline would never know. Would she? Maggie slowed down, her mouth began to open. Caroline slowed down too, her eyes darting around, panicked and searching. Could she sense her, could Caroline sense her?

. . .

Once, when Maggie was still reading to Caroline, they went out for coffee. As Caroline and she left the room, instead of grabbing her cane that was propped against the door, she reached for Maggie. Maggie had stiffened. It shamed her that she stiffened, but she just did. It was involuntary. And then Caroline said, "People don't want to help me because they think I don't need it, or they think it's condescending or something." Maggie had felt that way, felt that it would be obsequious, or belittling, to offer to guide the girl. Caroline was so proud. So off-putting. "But I want the help. I want people to guide me sometimes. I want a break from trying, from being afraid of what's out there, a break from all the things that want to hit me in the face. I'm alone in my world and I can't see. I need help." Maggie had loosened her arm by then, her initial stiffening giving way, and Caroline, sensing that, grabbed it all the more roughly. Maggie would do her best to guide her through the streets, but she worried. What if Caroline still bumped into something? What if Maggie didn't guide her as smoothly as she should? What if a crack in the sidewalk made her trip, a crack Maggie didn't see? It shouldn't have mattered, but it did. To Maggie, and to Caroline as well, thought Maggie, as the blind girl's face was screwed up in disappointment and resentment already.

Maggie stepped toward the curb. Commonwealth Avenue was full of cars. She couldn't cross. She couldn't escape. She could only pass her, face her really, face her, but not, because Caroline couldn't see Maggie. Digging her chin even deeper into the rough collar of her coat, she stomped by the blind girl.

It was the cold, thought Maggie, it was just too cold to be bothered with anyone, she told herself. But that wasn't true, and she knew it. In that moment, she had passed up a gift. A chance, a real chance—to grow, to regain her love—it flew up in a mad gust of air and disappeared into the frigid and howling Boston sky.

• down the alley •

HER RIGHT NIPPLE BURST, POPPED OUT LIKE A TIGHT WAD OF BUBBLE GUM, A PINK SWELLING THAT FELT ITCHY. She scratched it relentlessly. She was a scratcher, a fidgeter, a pen chewer. She had two chicken pox scars on her forehead from six years ago.

"Don't scratch! You'll get scars," her mother had warned, swatting her hand. Polly would run upstairs and crouch in a corner of her room and scratch and scratch until her forehead bled and she'd lick the warm, metallic blood off her fingers.

That was before she knew how to say "fuck you." But by the time her nipple turned into a mosquito bite, she knew how to say it. It was early fall, and Polly had just started at Jefferson Junior High, one of five hundred seventh graders who roamed the halls in a din of shouts, constantly vigilant of getting tripped, smacked, or spit on. It was 1986, in South Bend, Indiana.

Polly was a skinny little white girl. Every day she learned new things at Jefferson. "Hey you little white bitch! Want to suck my dick?" said a big black boy, as he grabbed his crotch. He was probably fifteen, and the size of a grown man. This was in the yard, after lunch, in her first week. Jefferson was full of children who repeated grades numerous times. Later that day a girl told her, "You look at my man like that again, and . . ." The girl made a motion at her neck. Then she pulled out a pocket knife. "You get it?" The girl was white, but from a different part of town. Polly had no idea who her man was. Maybe the boy-man whose dick she didn't want to suck.

The first time she told her mother to fuck off, her mother was sitting on the dirty blue velvet couch, reading the newspaper. Polly walked into the living room, excited. Her mother didn't look up. There was a bottle of beer, open, mostly full, sweating on the table next to her.

"Fuck you!" Polly said, clenching and unclenching her fists.

Her mother looked up, alarmed, but without missing a beat, she whacked Polly across the face with the newspaper.

Polly ran. First she ran outside, into her backyard, and then she ran down the alley. At the end of the block, at the end of the alley, was a field. It was an empty corner lot, the only empty lot on the square block. All during her elementary school years the neighborhood kids played kickball, kick the can, and tag there, especially during the summers. They also climbed the boysenberry tree and ate its berries.

Polly climbed the tree. "Fuck you," she said, picking the overly ripe berries still left on the branches at the end of September and eating them. Soon, she was calm, her lips and cheeks and fingers stained a gorgeous wash of purple.

. . .

"Your father's a faggot."

It wasn't the first time she'd heard that. This came from Michael Turley, who lived across the street from her. He was her age, a light-haired, thick-bodied boy she'd known since birth. She played with him often over the years. He was, in fact, her first sleepover. She remembered being able to take a bath with him; they were only five. It had been exciting in an innocent, five-year-old way, splashing around with a friend. A few years later, they had a day of playing gone bad.

"She showed me her butt," he shrieked to his mother, pointing at Polly. Mrs. Turley didn't do anything—she had five other kids to worry about—but after that Polly didn't like to play with Michael. Yeah, she showed him her butt. How dare he tell on her.

Regardless, they were neighbors. It was Saturday. Another dreadful week at Jefferson was over, and the month of September marched on. She was sitting on her bike, bored. Michael had lazily crossed the street to say that to her. Polly stared at him.

"Fuck you," she said and stuck out her middle finger.

"He's a fag. That's what my dad says. And you're an ugly flat-chested bitch."

Polly rode her bike down the street. The fire station, which sold candy as a sort of fundraising, was three blocks away, across from her old elementary school, and it was open for a couple of hours in the morning on Saturday as well as for an hour during the week after school let out. She rode slowly. It was a gorgeous day, sunny, the Midwestern sky flat and endless above her, clouds floating by like they had all the room in the world. When she got there she hollered up the stairs, up through where the poles came down through cut-out circles in the ceiling, "Candy Box!" Then she waited.

A fireman came down, keys clanging. His shirt, untucked, hung over his large belly. Polly's eyes were focused on the metal locker, which was full of candy, but he grabbed her chin and she looked up at him.

"I bet you got candy in your box, little girl," he said, and then he smiled, showing his red thick tongue between his teeth. His hand came out and tweaked her mosquito bite that pushed on her tight green T-shirt.

"Ouch," she said, putting a hand over her nipple.

"Don't like it? Wear a bra," he said.

Then he opened the locker and in that moment, as the door swung open, everything that bothered Polly went away in a wash of color. There were Reese's Peanut Butter Cups, Milky Ways, Snickers, penny gum, Twizzlers, Peppermint Patty's, Jolly Ranchers, Mounds Bars, Mars Bars, Almond Joys, Paydays, and SweeTarts. There was everything a girl could want. She bought a pack of Twizzlers and rode over to McKinley's playground. There were two black boys playing basketball and no one else. She parked her bike over by the hopscotch area and sat on some cement steps, carefully peeling one Twizzler off at a time. She gnawed away, happy to grind her jaw. Was her dad a fag? He was different. For instance, he didn't have a job. Maybe that made him a fag. He was gentle, too. He wasn't prone to smacking her across the face with newspapers.

A week later, her other nipple burst. She'd finally gotten used to the one little mosquito bite, had finally stopped scratching at it, and now this. In math class, she was going crazy with the need to scratch the shit out of it. She rubbed her notebook, hard and fast, over her chest. She was in the back row. John Bellini sat next to her, a short Italian boy from her part of town.

"What the fuck are you doing?"

Polly stopped rubbing the notebook against her now burning burst nipple. Her face turned red from embarrassment, from exertion. "None of your business."

"You're disgusting."

"Fuck you," she said to him.

He looked her squarely in the eye. Then he spit, slowly, a large wad of spit onto the floor next to his desk. Polly then spit herself, an equally large wad next to her desk.

"I bet I can make a bigger pile of spit than you," he said.

"Betcha," she said.

In the weeks that followed, Polly and John continued their effort, every day a different puddle. Neither of them ever declared anyone a winner, but it made the time pass. Finally, the teacher, Mr. Rotterman, noticed.

"Hey! Hey! What's going on there!" He was on them now, from the blackboard at the front of the class to the two of them in the back in a heartbeat, grabbing John by the arm and pulling him away. "Go to the principal's office. Now," he said. And then to Polly, "You. You I'll talk to after class."

The bell rang. Everyone left. The room seemed enormous, empty like that. Mr. Rotterman, from behind his desk, said, "Come here."

Polly sat still.

"I said, come here." His voice boomed across the room, echoing off the tiled floor, the empty white walls.

Polly stood up and then stood on her chair. She felt tall this way. She was tall this way. "No."

"I don't want to call your mother. But I will."

Fuck you, Polly thought. *Fuck you*, she thought, hopping down from the chair, her feet thwacking the floor, like a capgun sounding off. She walked to the desk. She was wearing a pair of white corduroys, and they were too small. They crawled up the crack of her front and back. They also didn't reach her shoes—floods, they called them. When she got to Mr. Rotterman's desk, he grabbed her, quickly, and leaned her over the desk.

"That," he said, as his hand slapped her ass hard, "is for being bad."

"Bad, bad, bad," he repeated as he spanked her over and over again.

. . .

Fall turned to winter and Polly had a friend. The friend didn't like her very much and wasn't nice to her, but Polly was so grateful that none of that mattered. Her friend's name was Breanna and she was from the other side of town, a skinny white girl, much like Polly herself, but one whose parents were divorced and one who was allowed to watch as much television as she wanted and eat sugar cereals for dinner.

Once, during a Saturday night sleepover, while they were watching the dancers gyrate on Solid Gold, Polly said, "Mike Turley says my dad is a fag."

"Really?" Breanna grinned and looked at her with interest. Generally, anything that caused another person pain or humiliation interested Breanna.

"Yeah. Maybe we should kick his ass."

"Whose ass? Michael Turley's or your dad's?" Breanna nearly fell over laughing.

"Shut up!"

"Maybe your dad is a fag." Breanna started to guffaw. Then she smacked Polly's arm.

"How could he be married and have a kid if he's a faggot?"

"Fuck if I know. I don't anything about fags."

When getting ready for bed, in the bathroom at Breanna's, Polly stared at herself in the mirror. She opened her mouth and stuck out her tongue. She grinned. She had big teeth in a small head. She pulled down her underpants and looked at the dark wisps of hair forming. This was new but not as troublesome as her nipples. It was more hidden, and it didn't itch quite so much. She touched herself gently, just there where the hair was growing in. Then she looked at her teeth again. When she was a little girl and her teeth were coming out, she could barely stand the feeling. The agony of waiting! It was like her other itches. She would tie dental floss around the tooth and saw, saw away. Back and forth, saliva, then blood, and still the tooth wouldn't come out. Her mother would say, "It's barely loose! Wait until it's looser before you pull it out." But Polly couldn't wait. She tried tying the string to a door and slamming it, but that didn't work. She always moved toward the door inadvertently. So she'd sit back down on the couch, sawing away, cartoons on in front of her that she barely watched because she was so intent on her sawing. And when it came out! Shooting across the room, smacking the TV dead on. The relief of it! The tooth was long and strange looking, because the root was still on it. Blood poured into her mouth, dripping down her chin onto the rug. She could feel her mother's anger. Looking into the mirror, she'd see the gaping, throbbing hole and it gave her a sort of satisfaction, but it was never long lived.

Over the Christmas break Polly's mother announced she was taking her bra shopping. They drove out to the mall to the Hudson's Department Store. The lingerie section was pink-walled and brightly lit. Everywhere stood racks of enormous, stiff bras and panties that were so huge she could have easily stuck both her legs through one of the leg holes. What the hell was she doing here? Her mother hated shopping. It made her sweat, she said, and also dizzy. But here they were.

"Excuse me," her mother said to a gray-haired saleslady, "I'm looking for a training bra for my daughter."

"Oh, yes." The lady smiled at Polly. "Right over here."

The training bras were white little things with triangle shaped cups on a rack that had a big picture of a girl smiling her ass off. Polly went into the dressing room and put it on. Her pale bubble-gum-sized nipples didn't come close to filling out the training bra. She understood that wasn't the point, the point was to hide her shame. Just the name of the bra confounded her. Training for what? Olympic boobs?

"Come out and show us!" the saleslady said.

"No," said Polly. She heard them whisper, then giggle.

On the car ride home, she asked her mom, "Is Dad a fag?"

"What? Jesus Christ! Where'd you get that?"

"I'm just asking."

"Your father is not a fag. For God's sake."

"Mike Turley says he's a fag."

"Mike Turley! That family has no class. All those kids and they're all wild and stupid. A woman shouldn't have more kids than she can take care of." Polly's mother's face was red now.

"Well then how come he doesn't have a job?"

They were at a red light. Her mother turned to her. "Your father is mentally ill. He's not a fag."

"Mentally ill?"

"Remember that time we visited him in the hospital? And he was making belts and little stools with stenciled paintings on them?"

Polly remembered. Her father making crafts, like a boy in shop class. She liked the stuff he made. It was nice. But that had been years ago, around the time of her chicken pox. She remembered he seemed quiet, but he was always quiet.

"You said he was sick. He was in the hospital."

"He was sick. Mentally sick. They gave him electroshock in the hospital, a hospital for mentally ill people."

The way her mother said mentally ill made Polly angry.

"He's crazy. Dad's crazy."

"Mentally ill!" Her mother screamed. Then the light changed.

When school started up Polly wore her training bra. She put little cotton balls in it to fill it out. But gym class was a problem. What was she going to do? Take off her training bra and let the cotton balls fall out? There she was, in the fluorescent glare of the locker room, stiff with terror. She had to get naked and get in the shower. She had no choice. The raging, lesbian gym teacher who sported a crew cut and weighed a solid two hundred pounds was yelling at everyone, herding them in and out of the cold hard spray of water with a fierce delight noticed by all. The bra came off. The cotton balls fell. Breanna was the first to point it out.

"Look! Polly stuffs her bra! Oh my God! Look!"

Polly ran for the shower, and like all the girls, crossed her arms over her chest. The girls laughed, they pointed, they grabbed her bra and the cotton balls and tossed them back and forth between each other. Someone smacked her arm when she came out of the cold spray, probably Breanna, but Polly was seeing white. The gym teacher hollered, "Everyone in, everyone out!" It was the only thing she ever said in the locker room. Outside of the locker room she had more sentences, like, "Get the ball. What are you doing? Get the ball!"

Polly stopped wearing the training bra. Her mother said nothing and probably didn't notice. Beer does that to people. Spring came and there was a fair at the Town and Country shopping mall right off the main strip, where teenagers cruised their cars high on dope and booze. The fair consisted of one small ferris wheel; a tilt-a-whirl; the very popular Himalaya, a fast ride that screeched out heavy metal music while it whipped everyone around forward, and then backward; a sawdust pit with a goat, a pig, and a spitting llama; and a food stand that sold corn dogs, soda, and cotton candy.

It was a Friday night.

"Mom, I'm going to the fair with Breanna and then spending the night at her house."

"Okay," her mom said, not looking up from the paper.

"I need some money."

"My wallet's on the table."

Polly went over to Breanna's house. The two of them

applied black eyeliner, mascara, and used her mother's curling iron. After they were all tarted up like miniature hookers, Breanna's mother drove them to the shopping center and dropped them off.

"Call me when you want me to pick you up."

"Okay."

Polly bought tickets for the both of them; Breanna never paid for anything. They rode the tilt-a-whirl twice, then they rode the Himalaya three times.

"She was a fast machine, she kept her motor clean," screeched the sound system. Polly's ear burned and the bass of the music thumped inside of her chest in an uncomfortable way. She was happy to be there with her friend. At the food stand, Polly ordered them a soda and a cotton candy. Three boys, high school age, with heavy metal T-shirts and mullets, came up to Breanna.

"Aren't you Angie's little sister?"

"Yeah, I'm Angie's little sister."

"Want to go for a ride?"

The girls looked at each other like they'd won the lottery.

"Sure," they said at the same time.

They all walked over to where the cars were parked. It was dark out, around nine thirty, and the air smelled of fumes from the rides and the rich pollen of spring. Lights from the ferris wheel glittered in front of them and crossed and bled into the lights of the cars coming up and down the strip. The smallest of the boys, a sandy blond-haired kid with bad acne, lit a small joint.

"It's just a pinner," he said, "but it's really special."

The stood in a circle, the five of them, and passed the joint around. At first Polly was intimidated, but she watched Breanna and did like she did. She held the tiny little white joint between her thumb and her forefinger and sucked real hard on it. The tallest of the boys said, "Damn, this is good weed."

The boy whose joint it was nodded, seeming pleased. The other one, a chubby sort, stayed real quiet and looked at Polly in a funny way. After the joint was smoked the oldest looking boy asked, "Want to go for a ride in my van?"

Suddenly, as if hit with a brick, Polly felt very strange. A fierce, hot energy surged through her body, from her feet to her head and everything went numb. She looked down to see if her feet were on the ground.

"My feet!" she said, "I'm floating."

Everyone laughed in slow motion. It was like a movie, where a camera slowly pans over a crowd, first Breanna next to her, then the tallest boy, then the quiet boy, his tight Poison T-shirt moving in slow motion over his stomach, then the little one with acne who had the joint, his wiry body bobbling while his feet grounded him. They were laughing so slowly, and now Polly couldn't hear them either, just see their mouths opening, their heads leaning back. *Maybe they weren't making any noise*, thought Polly.

"Let's cruise the strip," someone said. Polly wasn't sure who said it, but she was glad she was able to hear. Somehow she managed to get in the back of the van. Someone had helped her, had lifted one leg and then another, to make them crawl into the back of the van. She lay on her back and Breanna was next to her. The boys were in the front of the van; she couldn't see them. Occasionally she heard them say something: "Turn on the radio." "Give me a cigarette." There was laughter, lots of laughter. From where Polly lay in the back of the van, she could see out the back window, a blur of red and yellow lights. Her feet were not floating anymore. She looked at her arm and tried to lift it, but couldn't. What happened to her arm? She tried to turn her head to face Breanna, but she couldn't do that either. Somewhere deep inside her was a core of fear and panic, but it was wrapped tightly with layer after layer of fog and bewilderment. She tried to say, "Breanna," but nothing came out.

She heard the boys up front. Her ears worked. Her eyes could see. Nothing else worked. She heard one of them close to her now, as if his mouth were right against her ear. He said, "You've done been dusted, little girl."

Then there was quiet for a while. She stared at the lights out the back of the van. Again, she tried to say, "Breanna." It didn't work. Then a voice from far away said, "To Eric's house, motherfucker. It'll be a lemon pussy night! Drive, motherfucker."

Polly kept her eyes on the window. She had no choice really. But it soothed her, too, the blurry red lights. Like this, staring out the window, mesmerized, she fell unconscious.

When she came to, the van was backing up from her alley into a grassy part of the field. Polly wanted to say something.

This is the field, she wanted to say. This is my alley, she wanted to say.

Then she felt their hands on her. They were rolling her, rolling her out of the back of the van. She fell with a thud in the wet, cold grass. Breanna was next to her, but she wasn't moving either. She felt Breanna's cold arm against her own and it felt like the coldest thing in the world. She tried to move away from her friend, but she couldn't move. Then the van lurched forward, and she watched the red taillights and listened to the crunch of the wheels on the black gravel of the alley.

"*Meet me down the alley*," the song came to her, and she saw her father singing it to her, his eyes wet with tears. "Dad," she had asked, "can I go to the field to play kick the can?" This was before Jefferson, before her nipples burst, but after the chicken pox. "Sure thing, sweetheart," he said, and then he sang to her, his arms outstretched toward her as she ran out the door to go play. He sang, "*Come on and meet me down the alley, one last time . . . Come on and meet me down the alley, we ain't too young to die . . . Come on, meet me down the alley, to say goodbye.*" And she'd play and play, damp with salty sweat, running, hiding, kicking the can, relishing the scrape of metal on cement, her heart pumping fast, listening for those words, "*Olly Olly Oxen Free!*" She was down the alley, she was in her field. But it all felt wrong, because she couldn't move, she couldn't climb the boysenberry tree. The lights above her, the stars, pulled her eyes to them. They glittered just like the lights of the ferris wheel, like the coming and going lights of the cars snaking along the strip. She watched them, trying not to think how cold she was. She tried to turn her head to look at her friend, but she couldn't. And so she did the only thing she could do—stare above at the heavens and pretend they were the taillights on the strip.

· outsiders ·

RUTHIE WATERS ENTERED HER DORM ROOM AT LYNDON PREPARATORY ACADEMY WITH A SUITCASE FULL OF WRONG CLOTHES AND HEAVY METAL ALBUMS. She sported thick black eyeliner, a lumpy, obviously padded bra, and perfectly feathered hair. She was fourteen years old, from South Bend, Indiana, and when she spoke, her Midwestern accent marked her out. But all of this had changed by Thanksgiving. The curling iron she'd feathered her hair with was buried in the closet, the albums quietly placed in a Dumpster. She had tried desperately to speak differently, and eventually she had.

In Condon Hall, there were sixty girls: the lower mid class, to which she belonged, and the mid class, which was much larger. Her roommate, Alicia Camp, was the only black girl in the dorm. They were the only two not from Park Avenue or Greenwich. Ruthie's grandmother from Memphis was paying her tuition while Alicia was full scholarship. In fact, Alicia had grown up oftentimes homeless on the streets of Atlanta, her mother mentally ill, or occasionally taken in by her grandmother. She never knew her father. While Ruthie had very little in common with the Park Avenue girls, she didn't exactly have much in common with Alicia. And yet, they were both outsiders. Which was something.

That they had both been star students at their respective schools and now struggled at Lyndon was another. Alicia worked very hard and still got poor marks. This crushed her. Ruthie, not accustomed to working hard, fell in with a few girls in the mid class that liked to smoke pot all the time. She worked very little which never had been a problem before, but didn't do the trick at Lyndon. Nancy White and Melissa Carter, a year older than Ruthie but a lifetime ahead of her, lived across the hall and schooled Ruthie on how to smoke weed in boarding school, which was very different than standing in some alley in South Bend, passing a joint around.

They introduced her to the bong. What a wonderful device! They showed her how to use a hit towel. This involved rolling up a bath or hand towel into a tightly coiled tube, and after sucking down a bong hit, pressing your lips firmly against the towel to exhale. This left a perfect brown impression of lips on the towel, but kept the room free of the aroma of weed, which of course was necessary if one did not want to get expelled. And for all the bitching about Lyndon that went on, no one really wanted to get expelled.

One Friday night, after the hall teacher, a sour middle-aged woman named Miss Cranch, who was both the field hockey coach and a lousy math teacher, had checked all the rooms and turned in, Ruthie, as planned, snuck over to Nancy and Melissa's room. The bong hits of boarding school! There was nothing like it. The wealthy simply had better drugs. The weed was expensive and beautiful—tightly coiled balls of bright green with tiny threads of red in it. They all got incredibly stoned. Both Nancy, from Park Avenue, and Melissa, from New Canaan, wore Lanz nightgowns. Ruthie was in a pink T-shirt from JC Penney and her white cotton underwear. They all sat cross-legged on the floor in an intimate circle and whispered, just in case, but also because they were high as kites which for some reason made people whisper.

"We need to get you a nightgown," said Nancy, leaning toward Ruthie, her dark eyes focused but not unfriendly. She had the shiniest, thickest, black hair. Ruthie stared at her hair. She was beginning to understand so much at Lyndon. Like how the thickness of one's hair was a testament to coming from a "good" family.

"I have a nightgown, I just hate wearing it," said Ruthie. It was true, she had one. A synthetic fabric, embarrassing, nothing like the thick cotton of the Lanz nightgowns. Also, she always had hated wearing it; she preferred sleeping in T-shirts and underwear. "It gets all tangled up and I don't sleep well."

"Well, you could wear it when you come over at night," whispered Melissa, who then looked at Nancy. They giggled in silence. This involved putting their hands over their mouths and shaking ever so slightly while smiling with their teeth shut. Then they turned their eyes on Ruthie.

"It's just that we don't like looking at your underwear," said Melissa. She had waist-long hair, the color of wheat. It reminded Ruthie of a horse's mane. Suddenly, Ruthie missed her horse, very un-creatively named Sandy, back in Indiana.

This was one of those situations that Ruthie played one of two ways; one, she could acquiesce, acknowledging the superiority and rightness of her wealthier, more sophisticated friends. Or, she could play the tough girl from the wrong side of the tracks. The latter worked only some of the time. If it did work, she would garner some fear and awe. When it failed, she was met with either pity or repulsion, or some combination of the two.

"Deal with it," Ruthie said. She didn't whisper as well as she should. She was naturally a very loud girl, a Midwestern trait, for sure. "It's not like we don't all have the same parts. Don't be such prudes." Then she pointed at her crotch. "You each have one of these, too. Or at least I hope you do."

Nancy and Melissa looked stunned. Part of this was because of how stoned they were. Ruthie tried to read if it had worked or failed. Not that it really mattered. Sometimes, she just tried her hardest and hoped for the best.

"Whatever," said Nancy.

"Oh fine, I'll wear my nightgown next time," Ruthie said.

The following day was Saturday, a half day of classes at Lyndon. Ruthie was not accustomed to school on the weekends and it still was a terrible affront to her. She struggled through Advanced Biology, having entered because science had once been her best subject. Next came English, where they discussed Shakespeare's *Richard III*. Was he a bad man? Certainly it was a little bit more complicated than that. Or at least the ways in which he was bad were worthy of discussion. Her teacher was a kind, very tall Asian-American man named Mr. Lin. And lastly, Ruthie chewed her nails through Algebra. Done! She headed back to the dorm where she changed into jeans. Only on Saturday afternoons and Sundays were the children allowed to wear jeans. Thank God Levi's were a universally okay thing to wear. Alicia was at her desk, despondent over a textbook.

"Classes just ended, Alicia, give it a break!" Ruthie said as she searched for her cigarettes.

Alicia looked up from where she sat. "I'm going to fail. I'm going to fail everything and I have nowhere to go. I can't go back to Atlanta. You smoke pot all day with those rich girls, and you still get better grades than me."

"I wouldn't say I get very good grades," said Ruthie. She was getting all C's, except maybe in English and Art a B. This, after being a straight-A student in South Bend.

"You're not failing." Alicia turned back to her textbook.

"Ask for extra help."

"I have."

Ruthie didn't know what else to say. "I'm going to the butt room."

"I figured."

"I'll see you later."

The butt room was located in the basement of Condon Hall

right next to the laundry, which Ruthie greatly underused, as opposed to the butt room, which was like a second home to her. An airless, dingy room with three wooden benches and littered with cigarette butts, it had a pathetic fan that whirred on the ceiling. It was the only place the girls were allowed to smoke. Melissa and Nancy were there, puffing on Merits, which Ruthie switched to after being made fun of for her Kools.

"Ruthie, we're sneaking out tonight and going over to Bob and Jesse's room. You should come. They have a great weed and sometimes other stuff."

Ruthie wanted to hug them but then thought better. "Okay, what time?"

"Midnight, meet in the common room," Melissa said. She gave her long, straight horse hair a shake.

Midnight came and one by one the girls tiptoed down to the common room, across from the laundry room, spacious, with a few dirty couches and a small television. The windows were ground level. They all listened very carefully. Had anyone heard them? Was Miss Cranch on the prowl? After all telepathically discussing this through wide-eyed stares and deciding they'd gotten this far without getting busted, they carefully opened a window and looked outside. It was a hundred-yard dash to the boys' dorm. Ruthie noticed that Nancy was wearing deep red lipstick that looked amazing with her dark hair, and Melissa had on delicate blue eyeliner. Ruthie had given up on make-up altogether as her orangey base and black eyeliner were not a hit. She was having a moment of envy and awe. This happened a lot.

Melissa explained, "There's one night watchman for the whole campus. But we could get unlucky, so if it's all clear we still need to run like hell." And that is what they did, without coats or shoes, in the cool October night. It took minutes but it felt a lifetime, and soon the three girls were sitting on Jesse's bed, with Bob and Martin in the room, too. A tapestry hung on the wall, another over the window. Grateful Dead posters abounded, and the song "Sugar Magnolia" played gently in the room. The boys were less fearful. Their dorm monitor didn't give a shit. He was the junior lacrosse coach and very handsome. In fact, they claimed he occasionally got high with them. They didn't even use hit towels.

As perplexing as the girls at Lyndon were to Ruthie, the boys were from another planet. Jesse in particular had the most intense lockjaw. Ruthie often nodded while he talked, but really she had no idea on earth what came out of his mouth. Bob was a little more normal. At least she could understand him. And then there was Martin, a dark-haired, extremely tall boy. He most exotically was from Los Angeles, a place that Ruthie imagined was like a fairy tale from her childhood, full of strange things like dwarves and unbearable sunshine. Everyone gossiped how Martin was heir to a huge department store chain. And then there was the way they dressed. They wore incredibly baggy, ill-fitting, worn corduroys, tie-dyed T-shirts, and beat-up deck shoes which were in stark contrast to the tight jeans and cowboy boots the boys in Indiana wore. She found these boys effeminate, not just because of the way they talked, nor their slim builds—everyone was a jock in Indiana—but deck shoes? Girls wore them, too. She had never seen them before and yet everyone wore them with a sense of pride, especially if they were falling apart. This baffled Ruthie. Why would young men wear shoes that women also wore? Why were shabby things so cool? These were insanely rich boys. Why didn't they wear nice clothes? They wore suits when they had to, but otherwise they looked like pansy slobs.

The bong got passed around. Jesse said something, and Ruthie nodded. Soon, everyone was blind stoned. Martin leaned over and opened a package which contained dried up brownish things. "Shrooms," he said. Melissa and Nancy looked at each other nearly gasping for joy as they popped a couple of the gross looking things in their mouth.

"Come on, Ruthie," Martin said, lifting one of his bushy black eyebrows. "Don't you want to trip?"

Ruthie had never tripped and wasn't so sure she wanted to, but she was a curious, adventurous spirit, otherwise she wouldn't be in the boys' dorm, let alone at Lyndon. How many girls from Indiana choose to go to boarding school? Because it was her choice, unlike most of the students. She reached into the package and carefully chose two of the least disgusting shriveled mushrooms. Eating them, she focused on their texture, their musty taste, and then it was over.

What a mistake. Within half an hour everyone else was exploring parts of the room with awe and wonder, exclaiming about the beauty of it all, while Ruthie sat there rigid, seeing skeletons and blood instead of her friends, never mind her own legs, and the dark demons floating by and through everything visible. As the misery of her trip began to subside, the timid light of dawn shone through the tapestry covering the window. The girls snuck back, forgetting to worry about the guard and getting away with it. Ruthie spent Sunday in bed, only making it to dinner, and even that was a blur.

The following week moved slowly. In English class, Ruthie became confused about *Richard III*. He was such a bad man, but wasn't that because he was ugly and miserable? And how quickly things turned on him. One minute, he's the king and then he's all alone, without a single friend. This frightened Ruthie. The trip had made her sensitive, but not in a good way. She stared out the window, feeling a bit trembly.

"Ruthie? Ruthie, I asked you a question." Mr. Lin was standing in front of her.

"Oh, sorry, I spaced out," she said.

"Clearly. I'll repeat, what do you think about Richard's personal responsibility in regard to all the terrible things he did?"

Ruthie looked straight into Mr. Lin's eyes. "I actually was thinking about that."

Mr. Lin smiled. He didn't believe her.

"I just sort of got lost in thought about that. I was thinking how hard it is to be ugly, how hard it is to be an outsider, how it turns people cruel and bitter and mean. Richard is sort of super ugly, but even if you're just not what everyone else is, it makes you act in ways that you wouldn't if you were like everyone else.

Not that pretty people can't be mean, too. But that's not the point of this play. Anyway, he doesn't get away with his behavior, right? Maybe that was God's hand, as the end of play says. Maybe God had to take care of things because Richard had demons inside of him. There are demons, I do believe that. I've seen them." Ruthie raised her arms. "Not everyone can see them, not all of the time. I'm sure they change shapes, I'm sure they are shape-shifting demons. But I saw these brown ones, floating around and entering and exiting people without their knowledge. They were ugly and sought to hurt. I didn't see God. But who else could fight them?"

Everyone looked at her strangely and for a moment she was back to normal, noticing other people, noticing them noticing her. Was it because she said God? Probably saying she had seen demons sounded strange. She hid her religious background from everyone—her father was a deacon at the First Presbyterian in South Bend and she was forced to attend Sunday school her whole life—because she discovered no one else she was friends with was religious. It had been freeing, forgetting about God. But since she'd eaten those poisonous mushrooms, He was coming back to her.

Later that night, she sat in Melissa and Nancy's room, wearing her polyester blue nightgown that made her skin itch, expertly sucking down bong hits. The weed was making her feel much, much better.

"I think Martin likes you," Melissa said.

"Really," Ruthie said.

Nancy removed the hit towel from her face. "You should come to New York with us this weekend. You need to have your parents give permission to the dean, but you can totally stay with me—Melissa is. It'll be fun. Martin and Bob are going, too. They're staying with Jesse."

When Ruthie returned to the room, she told Alicia.

Alicia was sitting at her desk, studying algebra to no avail. "I wish I wasn't the only black person at this place. I miss my people."

The weekend was mind blowing. Ruthie had never been to New York. She had some vague idea what it meant to live in a penthouse on Park Avenue but to actually stay in one was a whole different thing. Nancy's parents were at their house in Barbados, another thing that was vaguely imaginable but also not, and they had the apartment to themselves, except when the extremely petite Chinese housekeeper in a blue starched uniform was there. It was one thing when she was sleeping in the "blue room" but another altogether when she had to sit patiently while the housekeeper poured her Cheerios. After she left the room, she asked Nancy, "Why does she pour the Cheerios? I can pour my own Cheerios."

Nancy said, without any real emotion, even with some patience, "Because that's her job."

That night, they were meeting the boys for drinks at the Plaza Hotel and then heading back to Nancy's presumably, since her parents were out of town. The girls had taken Ruthie shopping at Bloomingdale's, and Ruthie was wearing her brand new electric blue ribbed sweater dress. The only thing she liked about herself, her legs, were encased in black stockings that gleamed. She was so excited and overwhelmed she had to pee every five minutes for a while.

Being at the Plaza Hotel, getting served gin and tonics without having to produce a fake ID, was exhilarating. That's how the Plaza was, and everyone knew that except for Ruthie, of course. How could she know? She tried to control her excitement, tried to be blasé, which was not easy. The boys were in jackets and ties, and despite their usual boyishness that Ruthie found unmanly in comparison to the Midwestern boys she knew, they seemed quite sophisticated to her tonight. Ruthie had borrowed Nancy's red lipstick and sprayed Anais Anais perfume on herself, and even though she was in desperate need of a haircut, she felt okay about herself. Especially after the fourth gin and tonic.

All the little things that her posse took for granted made her wide-eyed and fragrant with excitement. Watching the boys act like men, hailing cabs for the lot of them. Watching them then open the doors, while the girls in their dresses, wrapping their coats gently around themselves against the fall wind, stepped primly inside. She had never in her life taken a taxicab. Nancy, eyes wet with liquor, telling the driver her Park Avenue address, arriving at this enormous beautiful building, the doorman in his gray uniform and cap deferentially opening the door for them. And then an elevator! Imagine taking an elevator that went

right into your apartment! The only elevator she rode in South
Bend was . . . well, she couldn't think right then. She was sure
she had ridden an elevator before.

They all nestled into the deep cushions of couches and chairs
in the living room, drinks in hand, passing around a lovely glass
pipe bursting with killer weed. Jesse pulled out a small white
package that at first appeared to be some uninteresting ori-
gami to Ruthie, and then it was clear that it was cocaine. Bob
whooped. Nancy fetched a mirror and Jesse expertly cut lines
with a razor blade that Ruthie was unsure from where it came.
She looked up from the pile of white powder, and Martin was
smiling at her. His eyes seemed particularly blue. She felt they
matched her dress.

"Ever do blow, Ruthie?" Martin asked, his elbows on his
knees, leaning very close to her.

"No," she said.

"I think you'll love it," he said.

He was right. Never had conversation been so urgent! Never
had she felt so confident! She belonged in this huge apartment,
with these foreigners who were her friends or something close
to that. Even Bob was interesting and engaging. He usually
receded into the background, but tonight his completely average brown hair and eyes and height and personality seemed
suddenly quite vivid. And although she always found Jesse a bit
sinister, he didn't scare her as much because, well, she was powerful, too.

She leaned over to do another line—it was her turn!—and

when she sat up sniffing and rubbing the tiny excess on her gums (she was a fast learner), Martin's face was so close to her she couldn't really see it all.

"Let's go to the blue room. You're staying in the blue room, right?" he said rather quietly. They'd all been sort of shouting all at the same time for some time.

After Martin refreshed their drinks from the living room bar that reminded Ruthie of an old movie she watched with her father years ago, she followed him to the blue room, where her sad little duffle bag laid on the ground, looking terribly out of place. He sat down and patted the bed next to himself. She followed obediently. He'd loosened his tie; it hung strangely down the length of his narrow torso.

They began kissing, their drinks sitting on the nightstand next to the bed. Ruthie had kissed boys in junior high, back in South Bend. In fact, in seventh grade, after smoking shitty weed in the alley behind her house with three eighth grade boys—how flattered she felt, why were they there with *her*?— she somehow found herself blowing all three of them. She remembered the feel of the gravel through her blue jeans, the feel of their dicks moving in and out of her mouth, the wonderful noises of pleasure the boys made. At the time, she felt powerful, as if she had this wonderful gift, as if they maybe loved her and appreciated her. Of course, this wasn't the case at all. She was ruined after that; no one would talk to her, except to call her a slut. This was one of the reasons she begged her grandmother to send her to Lyndon. But not the only reason. She was a girl who wanted out of South Bend, who wanted to kiss the department store heir in the blue room in a penthouse in Park Avenue. But she was not going to blow him, or anybody from Lyndon. It didn't work in South Bend and she knew it wouldn't here, either. The two places couldn't be more different but blow jobs meant the same thing all over the world, of this Ruthie was certain.

After a while, Martin stopped kissing her and pulled back, looking at her face. At this point they were lying on top of the bed and their bodies had mushed against each other some.

"Do you know what we have in common?" Martin asked, grinning, his eyes an incredible mixture of intense blue and bloodshot whites, hundreds of thin red lines intersecting around the blue. His mouth, grinning, was a loose, long thing.

"What?" She couldn't think of one thing.

"We're both outsiders."

"Because you're from Los Angeles?" This didn't make much sense to Ruthie.

"No. Because I'm a Jew. I'm not a WASP like everyone else at Lyndon."

Ruthie wasn't exactly sure what a WASP was, but she had an inkling. She'd had no idea that Martin was Jewish. The few Jewish people in South Bend all kept to themselves and owned car dealerships. "I didn't know you were Jewish. And I'm not Jewish. I don't get it."

Martin lay on his back now, right next to Ruthie who propped herself up on her elbow next to him, and his impressively large hands lay on his chest while he laughed softly, as if to hold onto his gentle laugh.

"Of course you're not Jewish. Even though Ruth is sort of a Jewish name." Ruthie thought about that. It was a Biblical name, she knew. Her father had named her purposefully after what he called, "the foremother of Jesus." Martin wasn't laughing anymore, just looking at her with those awful wonderful eyes. "You're *white trash*," he said. "And there are practically no other of your kind at Lyndon."

Ruthie got up, straightening her new dress, the dress she was so proud of, the dress she'd been so excited to wear. She picked up her drink. "I'm going to go do more blow," she said and walked out of the blue room, momentarily getting disoriented as to how to get back to the living room, stumbling a bit down the long, dark, endless hallway.

On the train ride home for Thanksgiving break, Ruthie sat by the window looking out at the world passing by her. It was dark, but she could make out shapes of houses, with their endless people in them, and a parade of scarily tall trees devoid of any leaves. She hadn't slept, her mind a storm of thoughts. The conductor had been kind enough, like the waiters at the Plaza, to serve her even though she was clearly underage. She had been slowly polishing off a bottle of red wine and she felt warm and woozy. Her thoughts, drunkenly floating through her mind, were of deep significance. It was a twenty-four hour ride to South Bend, and she was more than halfway there, the

Midwestern land flat and straight around her. Her once perfectly curled bangs hung limply over her eyes. *White Trash*.
She would never have a mane of hair to toss over her shoulder. She would never have a lot of things, she would never *be*
many things—but she wasn't the same person she was a few
months ago, no matter what anyone said.

The night before she left, she had persuaded Alicia to get
high with her. Alicia had never been high. They sat on the top
bunk, Ruthie's bed, and Ruthie schooled her on how to use the
bong, how to use the hit towel. Ruthie explained how sometimes, the first time you get high, you don't feel it, that you had
to try and feel it and then you'd see. Alicia said, "I don't feel it."

Ruthie said, "Take another hit," and Alicia did, her face all
concentration, all hard work, the same as she'd looked over her
desk all fall.

Ruthie was high, but she was always high these days. It wasn't
very special. Watching Alicia get high for the first time was new,
exciting even. "You're feeling it now, I can tell." Ruthie wrung
her hands in anticipation.

Ruthie looked at Alicia. She hadn't made one friend at Lyndon
that fall. She was the saddest person Ruthie had ever met. "Wow,"
Alicia said, her voice coming out in that marijuana-induced whisper. She leaned into Ruthie. "*I can see your shadow.*"

This startled Ruthie. She didn't want anyone seeing her
shadow. She didn't want to have a shadow. Without realizing
what she was doing, she slapped Alicia.

Alicia slapped her back, harder, and then climbed down from

Ruthie's bunk. The two girls lay there in the narrow beds, hearts pounding. Ruthie felt as though she could feel the vibration of Alicia's lifeblood coming up through the metal frame. Eventually, they fell asleep.

• cleveland circle house •

MARY HAD GROWN UP IN A HOUSE WHERE HER FATHER LOVED HER BECAUSE HE THOUGHT SHE WAS BEAUTIFUL AND BRILLIANT, AND HER MOTHER DESPISED HER FOR THE SAME QUALITIES. In truth, she was neither beautiful nor brilliant. She was an awkward girl, with a long torso and short legs, prone to nervousness, whose chin dropped too far down her neck. And although she was a hard worker, she never achieved better than slightly above average grades. She'd only been accepted to one college. But her father insisted on being proud of her, regardless. She was going off to college, in Boston. This was more than he had ever done.

It was 1986. At the very beginning of her freshman year at Boston University, she declared her major in psychology. This was partly due to her attachment to Larissa, a dark-haired, zaftig girl she met in Introduction to Psychology 101. Larissa had read Freud and Jung. Larissa impressed Mary immensely. The two girls decided that summer that they would get an apartment together in Allston and get jobs.

Mary called her father a week before she was to move into the apartment.

"Dad, I'm getting an apartment with a friend. We'll get jobs this summer and then stay in it the following year, during the school year."

"Is that allowed?"

"Of course, Dad."

"You're not coming home this summer? I'll miss you so much."

"This is the right thing to do, Dad. I'm going to try and get a job in my field, in psychology," Mary said, not knowing at all what that meant. "It's a good opportunity."

"I'll buy you a car," he said, quietly. "I'll buy you a car if you come home."

"Oh, Dad," Mary's face went hot. "I'm not coming home."

She'd been home at Christmas. She'd been looking forward to it and then was immediately miserable. Everything was exactly the same, but more so. Her mother's face shoved angrily in a newspaper. Her father bouncing around, trying to think of fun things to do, his hands in the air, saying, "Let's go to the mall!" For some reason, she'd assumed her absence would change things, would make things better. It hadn't. She ended up returning to Boston early. She had been nearly the only person in her dorm for two days, but she was just happy to be back.

The apartment was a small two-bedroom in an ugly gray building on the corner of Commonwealth and Harvard Avenues in the very center of the neighborhood of Allston. The first week, Mary would leap up the two flights of creaking, slightly mal-odorous stairs to their apartment, overcome with excitement. Her bedroom faced Harvard Avenue; it was noisy. Larissa got the back bedroom, equally small and dingy, but quiet at night. Larissa explained she got this room because she had found the apartment, which was true.

Larissa furnished the apartment within a week. There was a shiny red and silver 1950s table with matching chairs, vintage rock posters lovingly stuck on the walls with blue gum so as not to damage them, and a groovy purple velvet couch that barely fit in the tiny space that passed for a living room. No matter, it was all cheap, all second-hand and all fabulous. She had already found a job at a trendy record store on Newbury Street.

The night they both moved in, Larissa sat on the purple couch, stroking it with one hand. In her other hand, she held a cigarette. She had picked up smoking to lose weight and it was working. "Have you found a job yet?"

Mary let out a ragged breath. "I have an interview tomor-row. At a halfway house for formerly institutionalized mental patients."

"Really? That's fascinating." Larissa blew a smoke ring toward the ceiling

"I want a job in my field," Mary said.

The next day, bright and early, Mary put on her only nice skirt and a collared white blouse. She brushed her hair too much,

ripping the brush through it over and over so it ended up stat-
icky and wild, swirling upward and tickling her ears. She tried
to barrette it down with some success. Then she took the T
out to Cleveland Circle. It took about twenty minutes and was
above ground the whole way. The sun shone brilliantly, trees
swayed their green leaves in the light wind. It was June in New
England, she was interviewing for a job in her field. Her body
vibrated with the beauty of it, the possibility of it all.

She got off after the T had climbed a long, sloping hill that
seemed to be the end of Boston and the beginning of the sub-
urbs. The house was right there. Right in front of her. She was
forty minutes early for her interview and beginning to sweat. It
had suddenly gotten muggy. She hadn't noticed it in the cool
air-conditioning of the T. The house was a large, old Victorian,
with an enormous porch and two huge elm trees in the sloping
front yard. While she stood there staring at the house, a man
came out and sat in a chair on the porch and lit a cigarette.
She ducked her head and began walking and continued to walk
around until she was only fifteen minutes early for her interview, at which time she walked up the wooden steps onto the
porch. At this point, she was damp with sweat and there were
three men and one woman out on the porch, smoking. One
man stood nervously. He said something to her, but she couldn't
understand him.

"Hi, I'm here for an interview," she said. No one said anything. Perhaps she shouldn't have said anything. The woman
got up and went to the door just as Mary was going to.

"Brigid!" she screamed loudly. "Brigid!"

"Oh, excuse me," Mary said, trying to get past the screaming woman. "I'll just go in and find her."

Brigid came through a hall and it was suddenly clear that here was the woman she would meet and talk to, here was someone who worked here—indeed, here was the woman she spoke with on the phone when scheduling the interview and Mary had stupidly forgotten her name, had not written it down either—and that all the other people on the porch were "clients," as they were called.

"Hi, I'm Brigid. You must be Mary. You're early."

"Yes. Yes, I'm sorry I'm a bit early." They shook hands.

"That's okay. Come in here, to the office."

They entered a small room directly inside the house. "Sit down," Brigid said, gesturing to a couch. She sat at a desk and swiveled around toward Mary.

"I'll just explain a bit about the place. Soon, Ahmed should be here and he'll want to talk with you further. He owns this house and a few others. He's a psychiatrist. I'm basically the manager. I've been working here for four years," she said. "We have a weekly group meeting which either he or his wife attends. Usually his wife. The meetings, or sessions, are a part of the work week. In other words, you get paid for attending them. It's an important part of the job, actually. We all need to talk about how things are going, how it's all affecting us. The clients can be very tricky, behaving one way for one of us, another way for another one of us. Particularly the borderlines. They're the most tricky." Brigid smiled at this.

"I see," said Mary, but in truth, she was blinded with fear and could barely see Brigid sitting right in front of her. What the hell was she doing here? Borderlines? She had read about them. Read about them in her Abnormal Psychology class, in her DSM 3 manual.

Brigid took out a blue ice tray from a cupboard. "This is how we dispense the meds. See? Each one is labeled. You fill them up according to what they get. Changes are always noted in the med book, which is in this cupboard as well. We give out meds two times a day, morning and evening. And some can request an extra Xanax or something like that, depending. It's all in the med book. In the beginning, you'll always be doing your shift with someone who's been working here for a while, and usually that will be me. You won't be expected to do all this at once." She smiled at Mary. She had big, horsey teeth. She wasn't a pretty woman, but she wasn't ugly either.

Ahmed came in, smelling of cologne, his bald head the color of toffee. He took Mary to another office which seemed to be just his. Inside, the wooden floor gleamed and there was an expensive Afghan rug on the floor. It felt like a real psychiatrist's office. And it smelled nice. Walking through the house with him to get to his office, Mary had noticed an odor of urine and warm garbage.

"So! You want to work with the mentally ill! That is very brave of you. You will not regret it. Of course, I must ask you some questions about yourself," he said. His voice was deep and slightly accented, and he rubbed his hands together and smiled.

"Where are you from?"

"Outside of Pittsburgh."

"And you are a student at BU?"

"Yes. I'm studying psychology. I want to work in my field. I'm very serious about my . . . my career."

Ahmed smiled even more broadly. "Do you have a boy-friend?"

Mary hesitated. "No."

"Oh, you are so young!" Ahmed said, his thick hands thump-ing the desk in front of him. "Your whole life is ahead of you!"

"I guess."

"You must come over for dinner sometime. To our house in Newton. Yes, yes. You must." Then he paused. "I pay five dol-lars an hour to someone like you."

"Someone like me?"

"Yes, a student. Later, I may give you a raise. Okay?"

"Okay."

Then he began talking about himself. How he came from Morocco, how his wife was a psychologist, how they came to own and operate these homes. How in the past decade, the institutions were emptying out due to the great strides in medi-cation and treatment and now half-way houses were the way to take care of these people. How they were so much more "civi-lized" than the large mental institutions.

When Mary got home it wasn't quite yet noon. She went straight to her room and fell asleep for three hours.

• • •

She started work the following Monday. She arrived early, but not so early that she had to walk around for half an hour. Brigid was there. Brigid would work with her for the first few days. This comforted her.

This time, she stopped and said hello to the same group of smokers that were there on the day of her interview, and introduced herself.

"Are you going to work here?" a man with a mustache asked. He sounded angry.

"Yes."

"I'm Carol," the woman said, her voice breathy and raspy from smoke. "Nice to meet you." Carol's face was pockmarked. Her hair was greasy and she was very overweight.

"Nice to meet all of you," Mary said and entered the house.

Brigid was in the office with the door open, dispensing meds. A few clients waited patiently as she scooped out a number of pills and put them in their hands.

"You're early."

"Sorry."

"Don't apologize," Brigid said, as the last person waiting took their meds. "You like to apologize, don't you?"

"I don't know." Mary reddened.

"You know what they say about people who are early?"

"What?"

"They're anxious. Early people are anxious, on-time people are obsessive compulsive, and late people are hostile, or passive-aggressively hostile."

"I never read that in any of my psych books."

"I bet you haven't. "

The shift was eight hours, from nine until five. She also would have a night shift once a week, which was six hours long, from five until eleven. At that point, the house was locked up until the morning. Brigid introduced her to all of the clients that were lingering around, showed her the rooms they slept in, the bathrooms, the two common rooms. One of the common rooms, on the ground floor, had a television set turned on at all times. This was where the majority of the clients hung out. Toward the end of the shift, Brigid took her in to the office and closed the door.

"So, what do you think?"

"Well, it all seems fine." Mary didn't know what to say.

"I'll write in the log book, but I thought you might want to know how that goes, or talk to me about anything you may have observed."

"Okay."

Brigid held the log book in her lap and swiveled the chair around to where Mary sat on the couch. "Well, I think Carol seems depressed. She's manic depressive and I think she may be cycling into a depression."

"What should we do?"

"Make note of it, for one. And then bring it up during meeting time."

This didn't seem like doing a whole lot. "Can we do anything for her?"

Brigid smiled. "Like what?"

"Well, treat her in some way?"

"We could maybe up her anti-depressants. Listen, I was going to assign you two clients to spend extra time with. Everyone here has two clients who they take out for coffee or something like that, about once a week. Of course, you can only take them out if there is another person here. But I'm often here, as you'll find out. If you are here alone, you can spend some time with them in their room. It's an hour a week, approximately. Would you like Carol to be one of them?"

"Okay." Mary didn't actually want Carol. Carol disgusted her. But that was what she was here for, she told herself. To help these people.

"And how about Bob?"

"The skinny man with the glasses?"

"Yes. He's a paranoid schizophrenic and he's also mildly retarded. We call that dual-diagnosed. He's a sweetie. He loves to go to the pizza place for coffee. Although, we're trying to cut back his coffee intake. Try and get him to get decaf. The caffeine makes him more paranoid, you see."

"I see."

By Friday, Mary felt ready for something and she wasn't sure what it was, but it turned out she was ready to get drunk for the first time in her life. Or at least, that's what happened.

Darrell and Clay were having a party. They, too, lived in Allston, a short walk down Harvard Avenue and then a few blocks into a tree-lined side street. Larissa's face was expertly powdered a dull white and her lips were painted red. She carried a vintage silver purse that shone in the summer night. She smoked a joint as they walked.

Besides smoking cigarettes, Larissa had begun smoking pot at night, which Mary found alarming, but fascinating as well.

"Want some?" Larissa held the joint out to her.

"No, thanks."

"You know, I'm thinking of switching to a film major next year."

"Really? Why? Why would you do that?"

"Because I want to make movies. I want to make *art*."

"Oh." Mary hunched her shoulders down, feeling terribly disappointed. "What about understanding the world? Understanding human nature? Or helping people?"

"I never wanted to help people," Larissa said, as they turned toward Darrell and Clay's. "That's your thing. And I think I can better understand the world through art, through movies."

The party was big and loud. Music blared—The Cure, The Cult, Siouxsie and the Banshees, The Smiths, Meat Beat Manifesto. Outside of Pittsburgh, where Mary grew up, people listened to Foreigner or Van Halen. To rock music. Just being in the room with these people, the music playing, made her feel sophisticated. The room was filled with smoke and Mary kept going back to the keg.

"My father loves me so much, he offered to buy me a car to

come home. I said, no way. I'm staying in Boston," she said to three or four people at different times.

"Why does my mother hate me? Why? I never did anything to her, I didn't," she said to Darrell, at around two in the morning. They were sitting on the couch and she was leaning into his shoulder, feeling very emotional. It felt good, to be so full of feeling. Such tragic feeling! The party was over. Only she and Larissa remained. And Larissa had disappeared into a bedroom with Clay.

Darrell looked down at her. He was taller than her. This fact alone made her heart surge with a sort of love for him. He tried to say something, but he was too drunk and his mouth just hung open for a while.

"I think my father would sleep with me if he could. I think he loves me that much," the words came out, dirty and awful. The next morning, waking on the very same couch at Darrell and Clay's house, she would remember saying those words, and her head throbbed viciously with shame.

Monday at work, Brigid said, "Why don't you take Bill out for some coffee? Try to make it decaf, okay? But be back in time for the staff group meeting at one." She handed Mary three dollars.

Bill was standing in the TV room, watching the television with the sound off. He stood back in the corner, wringing his hands. He was an exceptionally thin man, tall with gray hair. His head lolled to the side and he wore very thick glasses. He was the sort of person that by looking at him, you could see that something was wrong with him. Not all the clients were like that, but many were, if not most. Some looked normal and even acted semi-normal. Bill looked wrong.

"Bill, would you like to go out and get some coffee?" Mary asked.

He turned his head to her. "Sure," he said. His voice was thick and slow, ruined by cigarettes and medication.

It was a lovely day, warm and clear. They crossed the wide expanse of Commonwealth Avenue and turned down to Brighton Avenue where there was a pizza shop. Inside, Mary ordered two coffees, both decaf. She felt embarrassed to be here in public with this man; she felt like the young men behind the counter were looking at her strangely. They sat down together at a booth and Bill lit a cigarette.

"They know me here. I come here a lot," he whispered.

"Oh? That's nice," Mary said.

"Sometimes, they give me the evil eye."

"Excuse me?"

Bill scrunched his forehead and leaned over the table toward Mary. His eyes looked exactly the same behind his thick glasses. "This," he said. "They do this." Then he sat up. "But I'm not afraid of them. It's just a message. I get messages all the time."

"No one is giving you any messages, Bill," said Mary. "People may look at you a little oddly, but it's not a secret message. I think shaving would help. A clean-shaven face gets less looks."

"I don't like to shave," Bill said, rubbing his face which was covered with erratic gray stubble. Then he leaned over the table again. "The beard protects me. It protects me from them knowing who I am."

"It's okay that they know who you are. You don't need protection. Really. You're a good man, Bill. No one is out to get you."

He laughed gently. "You're young. You don't know anything."

This made Mary blush. "Tell me about yourself," she said, trying to change the subject. "Where are you from? How long have you been living at Cleveland Circle House?"

"I'm from Waltham. I've been in Cleveland Circle House for four years, ever since I got out of the state hospital."

"Do you like it here? I bet it's nicer than the hospital."

"Sure. There aren't as many crazies here. I don't like the crazies. I know we're all a little crazy, but they had the real crazies in the hospital. I like it here."

Bill stood up and went to the counter and Mary watched him. He got a refill of coffee and sat down and lit another cigarette. "I hate decaf. I like the real stuff."

"Brigid doesn't think the caffeine is good for you, Bill."

"I know. But what's a man to do? It's my only fun. I don't drink beer anymore. I don't have any ladies anymore."

Mary didn't know what to do. To grab the cup away from him seemed cruel. And she didn't think she had it in her to do that, anyway. Who was she? A young college student. He was a grown man, regardless of everything else.

As they walked back quietly, she said, "I enjoyed talking with you, Bill. Anytime you want to talk, or need to talk to someone, you can come and get me. And try to remember, no one is out to get you."

"That's nice," he said, as they walked up the porch steps. "You're a pretty girl. I like you." And then he patted her on the shoulder.

The weeks passed. Mary learned how to fill the ice cube tray and made sure that everyone took their meds. As time went on, the futility of it all made itself aware to her. Would telling Bill that no one is out to get him ever convince him otherwise? Of course not. He had his delusions long before he met her, and most likely, he'd have them until he died. Mary began to focus on the practical, like Brigid, like all the others who worked at Cleveland Circle House. She tried to make sure the clients were all shaved and showered. She wanted their shirts tucked in. She wanted them in clean clothes. She wanted the bad smells to go away. She wanted them to do their chores and brush their teeth. The wild mood swings, the delusions, the overwhelming sadness and rages and fears—what really could be done about those? They came and went, taking over people and then setting them free. The blue and white and pink and red pills Mary doled out seemed to help some. If nothing else, they dulled the whole experience of life for them. Mary began to think that that was the best that could be done. To mother them about their daily life, and to medicate them so they didn't feel so deeply.

It was the middle of August, a Monday, and the group session was being led by Ahmed's wife, Laura. Brigid was there, like always, as well as a graduate student named Dave and another man, Roger, who worked there but also lived in another one of Ahmed's houses. He had been a client, but now he worked there. This gave Mary a sense of hope—They can be healed! They can get better! Normal even!—but she also kept her distance from him. She was ashamed to admit it, but he frightened her.

Laura was a petite brunette, with a very gentle voice. She began the group often by asking someone to "share," and then the person to the left of that person would share, and so on, until everyone had shared. Today was different.

"I wanted to start by sharing myself," she said. "My sister had a baby who died this week. The baby was born dead. It was a full-term baby. She named the baby Alexandra and there was a lovely funeral for the little angel. She also was able to hold her little girl. I was there at the hospital with her husband to witness the birth. You see, we didn't know at first the baby was dead, not until after we arrived at the hospital. She asked me to take pictures of her holding Alexandra, which at first . . ." Here, for a minute, Laura faltered. "Which at first bothered me. I guess I thought it was too much. Or something. But I did what my sister asked. What else could I do? In her moment of grief and sadness? I felt obliged to give her at least that, to honor her wish. So I took a picture. And then she asked me to hold her daughter and her husband took a picture. And I took a picture of her husband holding the girl, too."

The one rule about group was that no one was allowed to

say anything to the person speaking. Everyone just listened and then when the turn ended, everyone else just said "thank you." It was non-judgmental. It was just a place to share.

Laura reached in her purse. "As the days passed, I became less upset by my sister's request. I now really understand it. This was her daughter, dead or not. She was going to remember her forever. Why pretend not to? The days of trying to forget these things are thankfully over. No one forgets giving birth to a dead child. No one ever has, or will."

"Thank you," said Dave.

"Thank you," Mary said, out of obligation.

"I'm not done yet," Laura said, a hint of peevishness in her voice. "I brought the picture of myself holding Alexandra here to share with you all. I am going to pass it around. I, too, am grieving the loss of my niece. And I would like to share my pain here. That's what group is for."

Mary's head felt very light and her ears started to ring. The picture came around and she looked at it. In it, Laura looked down at the blue infant in her arms, not at the camera. Self-consciously, Mary held onto the photo for a moment, attempting to disguise her fear and disgust.

At the end of the session, they all took turns hugging each other. They often did that, but sometimes they did some other kind of "touch" therapy. Mary truly hated this part of the sessions. Just because they worked together didn't mean they should touch one another. She didn't understand the logic of it. As Laura came toward her for their hug, Mary gritted her teeth.

Slap, slap! She imagined slapping her, not hugging her. Then she hugged her.

The next week Mary's father called.

"I'm coming to visit you! Before school starts. I'm coming next weekend."

"Is Mom coming, too?" Mary asked, surprising herself with the bitterness in her voice.

"She doesn't want to," he said flatly. "But I'm desperate to see you, Mary. It's been too long!"

A flash of memory from Christmas passed through Mary's head. Her mother's back to her, angrily doing the dishes. Her father, wringing his hands, asking, "What record should I put on, Mary? What would you like to hear?"

"You'll have to stay at a hotel," Mary said. "We don't have a lot of room here."

"Okay. That's not a problem." He sounded hurt. Mary's heart flooded with shame. She was hurting the only person who'd ever been good to her. But the truth was, their apartment was too small and Larissa smoked so much weed now that there was no way her father could stay.

"Great, Dad. Call me when you get here."

The day before her father arrived, Mary was working her only night shift. It had been a relatively quiet night, except for Carol, who roamed through the common rooms, the hallways, and kitchen, and then did it all over again. And again. Muttering to herself, her hands balled up in fists. She had clearly cycled out of her depression. Something else was going on now.

It had been weeks since Mary had spent a special hour with Carol. She never missed her weekly coffee with Bill. She liked Bill. But she'd been avoiding Carol. Mary walked into the common room where Carol was at that moment.

"Carol," Mary said, but Carol ignored her and tried to walk past, muttering angrily. "Carol, wait." Mary followed her and grabbed her shoulder.

Carol turned around quickly and Mary drew her breath. Carol was breathing heavily, her face contorted with rage, her lips pulled back, revealing filthy teeth. For a moment, Mary was afraid.

"Carol, would you like to talk with me? In your room? I'm the only one here tonight, but I thought we could spend some time together here, at the house."

"*Oo kaay*," Carol said, with a nasty, fake enthusiasm. "Okay, miss pretty. Whatever you say, miss pretty."

"Come, let's go to your room. You seem angry. Let's talk."

"But of course, miss pretty. You're the *boss*," she hissed. "Aren't you?" But she began walking to her room.

Mary followed up the stairs. Carol shared a room with a very old woman who basically lived in front of the television. When Mary first started working at Cleveland Circle House, she read lots of the files on the clients. Barbara, Carol's roommate, had first been institutionalized in 1957, at the age of fourteen, for "promiscuity." She wasn't in the room when Carol and Mary

got there. Carol walked up to her dresser and grabbed a tube
of cream.

"I want to be pretty like you," said Carol, her voice falsely
sweet. "Will you help me? Put this on me. Help me put this
on," she said, and gave Mary the tube of cream. It was a reti-
nol cream, for her acne. Mary had helped her apply it before,
during one of their special hours. It was something Carol liked
to do.

"You should wash your face first."

"*You should wash your face first*," Carol mocked. Then, darkly,
"*Bitch*. You're a *bitch*."

"You shouldn't call me that, Carol. I just think it works better
if you put it on a clean face."

"What's so dirty about me? Huh? You think I'm dirty? Cause
I fucked your precious Bill today? I did, you know. I fuck every-
one here. You think you're so *pretty*. Don't you? Don't you?
This is what they like," she said, grabbing her enormous breasts.
"They like this, you see? You see?"

"Carol, I'd like to give you an extra Valium. I'll be right back.
Wash your face. We'll put the cream on. And . . . brush your
teeth. I'll be right back."

Mary ran down to the office. There was a beeper number
for Ahmed, to be used only in emergencies. There was also a
beeper number for Brigid. She called it first. She then grabbed
two Valiums and brought them upstairs.

Carol was laying back on her bed. Her hands were up her
shirt and she was massaging herself and moaning obscenely.

"Here, Carol. I want you to take these."

"No."

"Stop doing that. It's inappropriate."

"*Fuck you*. You think just cause I'm crazy I don't like to *fuck*? What do you know. *Bitch*. You've never been *fucked*, that's your problem."

"Take these," Mary said, standing there with her hand held out.

Carol took the pills and put them in her mouth. Then she opened her mouth wide, showing the two white pills on her tongue.

"Swallow them, Carol."

Carol stood then, groaning, sticking her tongue out defiantly, the pills still there, and she began massaging her breasts again.

"I said, swallow them." Mary grabbed Carol's jaw and tried to shut it. For such a big woman, behaving in such an intimidating fashion, she felt like Jell-O in Mary's hands and fell backward on the bed as Mary mashed her jaw together. Carol began laughing, muffled by Mary's hands, but laughing all the same. Then Mary stood back and slapped her, hard, across the face.

Carol sat up. "*Oooh*, you're not supposed to do that."

"Fuck *you*. You're a cow. A disgusting cow."

"*Oooh*, miss pretty said a bad word. You're not supposed to talk to me that way. *Tsk tsk*. I always knew you were *bad*." Then she began to laugh again.

Blood poured into Mary's face, the same blood that made her blush easily, the same blood that betrayed her nervous nature, that showed her easy shame, and she pulled back her arm and punched Carol's soft, greasy face, as hard as she could. A glistening circle of red appeared on Carol's mouth and began dripping down her chin. She cowered on the bed, looking momentarily frightened. Then she smiled.

"That was *wrong*. You did the *wrong* thing, missy."

The phone rang. Horrified, Mary ran down the stairs. It was Brigid.

"I think Carol is really manic," Mary said.

"Can you get her to take some extra Valium?"

"I'm trying, but she's not being very cooperative."

"Well, keep trying."

"I need help." There was a silence. "I'm afraid."

"She won't hurt you. She may seem menacing, but she's never hurt anybody."

"I think she should be hospitalized."

"Maybe I should come."

"Maybe I should call the hospital?"

"You could do that. Call an ambulance. I feel like I should be there for such a decision, but . . . do whatever you think is right."

The ambulance came in five minutes. *Maybe*, Mary thought, *no one will find out I hit her*. Or believe her. A crazy woman's word against hers. The two paramedics escorted her out as Mary stood on the porch. It was dark and unusually cool for August, although it wouldn't be August much longer.

"What happened to her mouth?" asked one of the

paramedics. He was holding Carol's arm, standing right in front of Mary.

"I don't know," Mary said, her right hand shoved deep in her jean pocket. "She's been out of control for hours. That's why I called you guys."

They walked toward the ambulance. Mary stood on the porch, watching them.

"*You shouldn't have done that, Mareee!*" Carol screamed at her, and then she disappeared in the back of the van.

The next morning, Mary met her father for lunch at an Italian restaurant on Newbury Street. There were red and white checkers on the tablecloth, and opera music played on a radio. They sat outside, but it was bit chilly. He leaned over the table, so close to her, his glasses slightly fogged from breathing too hard. His face looked creepy: he was getting old. Why had she never noticed this before?

"It's so good to see you," he said, reaching his hands out to grab hers. She pulled her hands away and watched her father's face fall.

"What happened to your hand?"

"Nothing."

"You look so beautiful, Mary." He put a hand on her shoulder. She shrugged him off. "What do you want from me?"

"Want from you?"

"Yeah?"

"I just want to see you, Mary. You're my daughter. I don't *want* anything from you!"

The look on his face! The pain! And it was all because of her. Mary got up and walked to the door.

"Mary? Mary!" He called after her.

That night, Larissa and Mary had a party at their apartment. Larissa bought a half keg and bottles of whiskey and vodka and laid out colorful plastic cups. She called everyone she knew. Mary did nothing, except help her carry stuff up the stairs and then help her arrange things; she pushed the kitchen table against the wall, as Larissa pointed her finger at her, telling her to do it.

"And I'd like you to chip in for the booze."

"Of course," said Mary.

Larissa stood there, looking thoughtful, one hand on her now well defined hip. She'd lost so much weight that summer that her once childish pudginess was gone entirely. Her dark hair, once short and framing her face, now hung in thick long curls around her shoulders. Her face had cheekbones that stuck out angularly and her breasts curved low on her chest, like a woman much older than nineteen. She was mesmerizing. Beautiful. Mary stared at her.

Mary set up the keg and pumped and pumped it. She began drinking before people arrived. She kept drinking once they did arrive. In fact, she stayed standing, next to the keg, drinking, until the keg was empty. She served other people, who came and went. The music was loud. The Velvet Underground, Joy Division, David Bowie. It bothered her. Why had she thought this crap more sophisticated than Van Halen? Why had she been so impressed? She longed for her room at home, with its bland furniture and posters of horses. She longed for the quiet of her small town. Stumbling, she went into her back room to lie down. People were sitting on her bed, talking. Other kids sat on the floor, their legs bent up so they could fit in the tiny space. She fell on the bed and passed out.

The next morning, the apartment was a mess. She knew she had to clean it. Larissa would tell her to. She thought if she cleaned up before Larissa woke, that it would make her happy. Her head hurt and her mouth tasted awful. While collecting cups filled with the dregs of beer and cigarette ashes, she felt bile rise in her throat. She went to the bathroom and threw up. When she came out, Larissa was standing there, wearing a dark green nightgown that went down to her ankles.

"Are you okay?" she asked, voice unfriendly.

"I got sick."

"I can see."

"I've been cleaning up after the party. The smell of stale beer and cigarettes made me ill."

"I think it was all the beer you drank. You drank half of that keg yourself. Now, can I get in there?"

"Yeah."

After Mary had finished cleaning the apartment she took a hot shower. She was supposed to work the next day. And it was a group meeting day, too. With a towel wrapped around her, she headed back to her room.

"I need to talk to you," Larissa said. She was sitting on the purple couch, smoking. The smell of the smoke made Mary's heart pound.

"Okay." Mary stood there.

"Go get dressed. Don't just stand there in your towel."

Mary headed into her room and shut the door. Larissa found her repulsive. She could tell. Funny how that was, how Larissa's body excited her, moved her, really. And she had the exact opposite effect on Larissa. She didn't look at herself as she threw on jeans and a T-shirt.

"That was quick." Larissa said, and it sounded like an insult. "Listen, you have to move out. Clay is moving in."

"What?"

"You have two weeks," she said and blew a perfect smoke ring.

"Where will I go?"

Larissa laughed. "That's your problem, honey. You know, you never do anything. You're so . . . so passive. This will be good for you. Force you to take some responsibility for your life."

"But the plan was to live here for the next school year—"

"The plan changed." Larissa interjected. "And you aren't on the lease, anyway."

"Why don't you like me?"

There was a pause, as if Larissa were really thinking about this question. Then she said, "What's there to like?"

"What did you ever like about me?"

"I don't know if I ever did."

"Then you're just as fucked up as I am."

"I doubt that," she said, dryly.

"*You don't know me,*" Mary said, and her voice was different than she'd ever heard it before. She lifted her bloody knuckles at Larissa. "*You don't know the half of me.*"

She ran out of the apartment, down the rancid smelling stairs, out onto the street.

On Harvard Avenue, the traffic was light. It was two o'clock on a Sunday. She looked wildly back and forth. She saw no one she knew. Somehow, this comforted her. Then she thought, what did she care if she saw someone she knew? What did it matter what anyone thought of her? She turned up Common-wealth Avenue and started walking toward Cleveland Circle, toward Cleveland Circle House. "*You shouldn't have done that, Mareee!*" Where would she go now? She kept walking until she came to a bus stop. There, she stopped and sat down. A bus came, and she got on it. It drove up the hill, toward Cleveland Circle. There was the house. She saw the smokers smoking on the porch. She wouldn't go to work tomorrow. No, she'd never go back there. The bus kept going, and Mary panicked. At the next stop, she got off. She ran to a pay phone.

Her mother answered the phone. "Yes, I'll accept the charges," her mother said, her voice familiarly stiff with barely suppressed rage.

"Mom. Is Dad back yet? Is he there? I need him . . ."

"No. He's there visiting *you*. Where are you? Why in God's name are you calling collect? Mary? Mary! Are you there!?"

Mary hung up. Here was a woman who hated Mary for some power she perceived Mary to have. Just like Larissa hated her for her lack of it.

She'd try calling the hotel. Maybe he hadn't left yet. He'd forgive her, he *loved* her. Yes, he did, and that was all that really mattered.

· pussies ·

"It's beautiful," I said without touching it, although I wanted to.

"This is my 'I'm never going to be a fucking bank teller' tattoo," she said, smiling. Her hair had recently been shaved into a military-like flat top and dyed white. Lise was much cooler than me. Her family had tons of money, so why would she ever need to be a bank teller?

I was her doormat friend. This was a good thing for me to be at the time, for various reasons. For one, it was the only way to be her friend at all. I treated her with adoration and she tolerated me and mocked me gently from time to time. As good as my adoration must have felt to her, it also felt good to adore her. It felt like love in my heart, like the unrequited love I once had for my older sister when I was seven and she was twelve. It felt a bit like my love for Ron, my boyfriend at the time, a drummer in a rock band, who wasn't a very good boyfriend.

Lise lived off of an enormous trust fund and had never held a job in her life. At the time, I was waiting on tables at an Italian restaurant on Newbury Street in Boston. I had come to New York to visit her. We had met years before, in a summer abroad program in Mexico during high school. Now, she lived in a spacious one bedroom apartment on the twenty-first floor of a doorman building on Sixteenth and Third Avenue. The windows held stunning views. I looked out at the fall sun, bright, but holding the chill of the air in it. I wanted to say, what's wrong with being a bank teller? But I knew the answer. It wasn't cool. It was being average. It was working for *the man*. It wasn't making your art.

"Well, it's beautiful," I said again, and I meant it. Mostly, I was jealous. I could never get such a tattoo. I needed to work and I had no idea what kind of work I would need to get in the future. Bank teller? It seemed better than sucking dick for a living. I was only twenty-two.

"Let's go shopping after I feed the cats," she said and put her coffee mug in the sink. She had two cats, one enormous, half-blind cat named Dave and a little thing called Susie. I did the breakfast dishes while she tended to her pets. Then we went out. It was a gorgeous day and the East Village was so different than Allston, the neighborhood where I lived in Boston. It was so much cooler, like Lise was cooler than me. It had a secret language I could feel, but couldn't decipher. I wanted more than anything to hold the key to its language. But in the meantime, I would have to walk around, craning my overly long neck around, absorbing the people and stores as they passed me by.

"Careful, Linda," said Lise, annoyed, as always, with my clumsiness. "You keep bumping into me."

The next time I visited her I was very sad. My boyfriend, Ron, had been treating me like shit. I'd been going out with him for two years and he was the first man to ever give me an orgasm. In fact, he gave me an orgasm before I ever gave myself one, so I was very attached to him. But he was an asshole. He had borrowed six hundred dollars from me and then hadn't returned my phone calls for two weeks. The last two days of those two weeks I had stood outside of his apartment at night, staring in at the light in his bedroom window, feeling thick with self-hatred. When he did call me back, he said he couldn't see me right now. That he needed his space. I had three days off in a row from work, so I took the Greyhound to visit Lise. She was good that way. She never turned me away. She let me visit.

"Check it out," she said, tilting her chin upward. She had a new tattoo on her neck in gothic style writing.

"Is that your name?" I asked.

"Yeah, man. It hurt so much. But it was worth it. It's so jail. No one is ever going to fuck with me now."

I tried to think of any time that anyone had fucked with her and I couldn't. She went to a posh private school, a Quaker school, in San Francisco. There were some stories of mean nannies. But still, her life always struck me as quite safe.

"Wow." I said about her new tattoo. "That is really rad."

Her live-in boyfriend, Dylan, who played in a punk band, was back in LA, visiting his friends from Crossroads, she explained.

"Crossroads?" I asked. "Isn't that a rehab?"

"No, Linda," Lise said, like I was the dumbest person in the world. "It's the school he went to in LA."

Because Dylan was out of town, I got to sleep in Lise's bed with her. This was an enormous treat for me. I could run my hands over her bristly yet soft, closely shaved hair. She was on the zaftig side. We would spoon, and my hands could touch her bosomy chest. She was like a big, comfy pillow to my angles and corners; my straight, bony body. I savored the closeness: I was so hurt then, so mad at my boyfriend and mad at myself for needing him to go down on me to get off. Before we went to sleep, we tented the blanket over our heads like children playing a game. Suddenly our warm, damp bodies blossomed into the bubble the tented blankets had made. We had entered another world, like children do. Oh, the intimacy! The heat of our bodies, our animal selves, safe and covered! We heard a tiny meow above us, felt the tender steps of little paws. Lise opened the blanket to let the kitty in.

"Come in here, Susie Q, come here, pussycat," Lise cooed, and in walked Susie. Purring, she slunk down to our feet and curled up. "You know, Dylan and I don't really have sex anymore," she said, her body a yellowish, hot fruit under the covers next to me. I felt her breathe. My eyes had adjusted and I could see her in that barely way.

"Really?" Ron and I fucked like poisoned beasts the times we were together. It was vicious. But we were seldom together anymore. "You two are such a great couple. Why do you think you don't have sex anymore?"

"We're like best friends. I don't know. We just have no passion or something. He's like my brother." She rolled over onto her back. It was getting stuffy now. It was the time when you throw the blankets off and feel incredible release. She turned back to face me. "Sometimes, I think it's because we started pooping in front of each other. Like that was the beginning of the end of our physical attraction."

"Wow. Maybe you should see a counselor. You two are so good together. Ron and I, we have sex. But we're horrible together."

"You're horrible together? He's horrible to you, Linda. There's a difference."

Then I threw the blanket off. It felt involuntary. The fresh air cooled my pink cheeks. Susie scurried out, gently rubbing her feathery self against my body as she went.

"You're right, Lise. You're right."

The next morning, we went shopping again. I never had that much money, but she had a credit card that her mother paid off every month, and shopping was something she did sort of like I waitressed. It was serious work to her. I tried not to bump into her while I excitedly walked down the street with her. I couldn't help but crane my head around: the East Village mesmerized me. Lise bought a pair of dark, stiff jeans, a forest green cash-mere sweater she claimed was for visiting her grandmother, and a vintage, yellow vinyl handbag. Then we stopped for lunch at a place on Sixth Street that we'd been to before. It was downstairs and had a lovely garden. A piano sat in the back and sometimes someone was there playing, but not that day.

"I'm a vegan now, Linda."

"What's that mean?" I asked.

"I don't just not eat animals, I also no longer consume any animal by-products. No milk, no milk products, no eggs, no honey, no leather," Lise went on, "I still haven't decided whether to throw out all my leather stuff I already have . . ."

"Wow. That's intense. That's a real commitment. No honey? I didn't think honey was so bad." I ate my salad in silence. I was not a vegetarian, but I sort of pretended to be one in front of Lise. I didn't actually ever say to her, "I'm a vegetarian!" but I never ate meat in front of her. So, in my mind, I was only being half-dishonest, as if such a thing existed.

"It's a matter of principle. The bees produce honey for their own reasons, not for us. We think we own this world, but we need to share it properly with other creatures," Lise said, the wonderful edge of righteousness emanating from her very core. "It's up to each and every one of us to make this world a better place. That's what it takes. To end the senseless killing of ani-mals by the selfish, hate mongering rich people in this world."

"Right," I said, thinking of all the bacon I planned on eating when I got back to Boston and feeling so confused yet so in awe, in admiration, of Lise. She knew what was right! And she even had the good sense to then live in accordance with her knowledge. I knew nothing at that point, not even how to get myself off, so her convictions and certainties amazed me. I wanted to be her, in so many ways. I wanted to be rich and so secure in my righteousness. I wanted to have large breasts and a boyfriend who was nice to me even though he was a rock dude.

Later, we decided to go hear a friend of hers and Dylan's band, Inner Revolution, play at CBGB. I was so excited. Seeing bands was the absolutely most favorite thing I did in Boston. And CBGB was this historic club that I had never set foot in. How would it compare to Boston's The Rat? I put on a pair of suede hot pants that laced up the sides and black vinyl (see! I was sort of vegan!) boots with chunky high heels. I'm sure I wasn't wearing a bra. I never wore bras.

Lise looked at me. "Are you sure you want to wear that?"

"Yeah, man! It's CBs! I'm excited. I've never been." Then I noticed her outfit. It consisted of dark rinsed, baggy jeans, high tops and a plain black T-shirt.

"Wow, the style is really different here, isn't it?"

"I guess so. You look sort of tacky."

I didn't know what to do. Put on my jeans? I felt that would be no fun and I was desperate to have fun.

"I'm just trying to rock."

"Whatever. Let's go. It doesn't matter."

. . .

The inside of CBs was perfect. Stinky, dark, dirty, graffitied. I wanted to jump up and down and go, "Woohoo!" Instead, I began drinking heavily. The music was so loud I could barely hear the conversations Lise had with her friends. I didn't really know any of them and I was feeling a little left out, a little self conscious, but it wasn't messing with my joy of being at CBs. The music was different than the bands I frequented in Boston: it was more serious, less "fun." They were saying important things. They were making a stance. They all looked like Lise, but they were young men. I liked my music sexy and angry. I liked a band called Zug Zug, which meant "fuck" in caveman, according to the guys in the band. One of the bands ended and I stood, swaying, next to Lise and a couple of other people. They gave me the sort of look that when drunk, you ignore, but the impression is there, the pointedness of it, and the next morning, while hungover, you can't get it out of your head.

"Dylan went to a party in Silver Lake and had a great conversation with Thurston. His band might open up for them on a few dates during their next tour," Lise said.

"That's cool. That's very cool," said a hunched over, heavily tattooed guy next to her.

"Who's Thurston?" I asked.

"Thurston *Moore*," the guy said. His voice lingered on certain syllables and he swallowed others. It took me a minute to recognize the "accent," but then I did: lockjaw. I'd met some other people from Darien or Greenwich with the same way of speaking.

"Who's that?" I asked.

"Uh, Sonic Youth, dude?"

"I think I've heard of them."

Everyone thought that was funny and laughed. Then they started talking about Drew Barrymore and I did know who that was, but I went to the bar instead and ordered another shot and a beer.

The next morning, Lise made coffee and brought it to bed. She snuggled against me and felt warm and smelled sweet with only a hint of staleness. I wanted to recoil. I felt vile.

"Thanks," I croaked.

"You were pretty shitfaced last night."

"Hell, yeah. Isn't that the point of partying at a rock club?"

"Listen, Linda. A lot of my friends are into straight living. You know? The straight edge scene? No meat, no booze, no drugs. I mean, that shit can ruin people's lives. It's not partying. It's just making bad choices."

I looked at the pile of trampy clothes next to the bed. "Sorry."

"Don't be sorry. But you might want to get your shit together."

Six months went by and my life in Boston got shittier week by week. I had begged Ron to take me back, on my hands and knees. I don't know what came over me. It was ugly. It freaked him out. But it didn't freak me out. I was proud to be so vulnerable, so honest. And I was a bit relieved to have made that one final effort. I felt so lost without him and I still couldn't get myself off, not that I ever tried very hard. I just wanted him. Then I heard he had another girlfriend. It was the thing I feared the most, the thing I had obsessed over—did he have someone else? Did he?—and when I found out he did, it set me free even more than the begging on hands and knees. Now, this setting free was not a one note sort of freedom. First it set me free of eating properly and taking care of myself in any way. Then it freed me to cry for hours at a time every day or so for about three weeks. But then it freed me in other ways. A lightness. I bought tickets to Buenos Aires. I was going to teach English there. And freedom has its high, even if you never wanted to be free in the first place. I was going to miss Boston, where people still ate bacon, girls at rock clubs dressed like they were going to a Led Zeppelin concert in 1971, and hangovers were savored slowly in bed all weekend long. But I knew I had to leave because it was Ron's town. That song, "It used to be his town, it used to be her town too," had been haunting me for weeks. Someone always wins and it wasn't going to be me. I was many things: young, hopeful, lacking cynicism, and unbeknownst to me, still able to adjust and change to all sorts of circumstances. But a winner I wasn't. Before going to Buenos Aires, I decided to visit Lise.

Dylan was in town so there was going to be no sleeping in her bed. I got off the bus and took the subway downtown from Port Authority. The doorman called up and I was "Okayed," so I took the elevator to her apartment. Lise and Dylan were lounging in the living room. It was summer, and even though it was 7:00 P.M., the light still shone through her impressive windows. I hugged Lise and then awkwardly hugged Dylan. I hadn't seen him in ages.

"So, how's it going, Dylan? How's the band?"

"It's going well, really well," he said. He was quiet with me. He wasn't quiet with everyone, this I knew. I felt a supreme lack of interest in me coming from him, and it was visceral, like he was a gay man who found women physically vile. Unfortunately, at that stage in my life, it made me pursue people all the harder. Like me! Like me! Find me interesting!

"Are you touring this fall?" I asked.

"Yeah, yeah, we got a van all lined up. It's gonna be tough. But it'll be awesome, too."

"Yo, Lise, check it out," he said. "I forgot to show you what I picked up when I was out earlier." He got up and walked out of the room.

Lise was lounging on her butterfly chair, her hair a brilliant white that elegantly framed her round head, her dress draping over her curves perfectly. She had one leg up on the side of the chair, which she kicked back and forth lazily. She gave me a look of excited anticipation and I returned it. Dylan was back in an instant, holding toilet paper.

"Look man, I lifted two rolls from the Kiev," he said. The Kiev was a diner around the corner.

"You are awesome, dude!"

This was one of my lost moments. Stealing toilet paper from

a diner run by working class Polish immigrants? Then I smelled something funny.

"Do you guys smell that?"

"No. What do you smell?" said Lise.

"I think I smell smoke."

"I don't think so," said Dylan.

We all listened to a song. He sounded angry and the music was very fast and you couldn't hear the words at all. But it had real emotion. Mostly the emotion of anger, or that's the impression it made on me, but it felt real, not forced or fake. When the song was done, I stood up. I was nervous.

"I smell smoke." I walked to the door, and sure enough, right when I opened it, a fire alarm in the building sounded. The hall was smokey. We were on the twenty-first floor. I shut the door immediately.

"Oh, God, oh God," said Lise.

"We've got to get out of here," I said. There was hysteria in my voice. Her apartment really smelled now. I could see smoke curling under the door. I walked nervously toward Lise and Dylan, who were standing silently. "Let's go. Now."

"The cats!" Lise said and went into the kitchen.

"Fuck the cats!" I screamed. And in that instant, I was full of regret.

Lise had grabbed two cat carriers from on top of the fridge. Tears moistened her round, round face. She stood there, shocked, confused. I grabbed one of the carriers from her and looked wildly about for a cat. I saw the big one, Dave, and grabbed him by the back of his neck and shoved him into the carrier with a forcefulness I didn't know I had.

"Stop! You're hurting him!" Lise wailed.

"Dude," Dylan said. "Not so rough."

"Fuck you, you fucking eunuch!" I screamed at Dylan. "You're just standing there, waiting for the staff to do everything!"

I dropped the carrier and looked about. Lise was holding Susie with the carrier in front of her and she was trying, and failing, to get the protesting cat in it.

"Come on, Susie, sweetie, that's a good kitty," she cooed.

I grabbed the cat like it was a sack of garbage and slammed it into the carrier, locking it.

"Let's GO!" I screamed.

Dylan was holding Dave, and Lise held Susie. We opened the door and there was smoke everywhere. Collectively, we didn't try the elevator. There were two sets of stairs and we went to the nearest one and opened the door. The smoke was white and thick and curled and moved. We ran down a flight, blinking, choking. Then we ran down another flight but the smoke was thicker and hurt our eyes, our lungs.

"Let's try the other stairwell," Dylan screamed over the fire alarm.

We exited on the nineteenth floor. The floor wasn't as bad as the stairwell and the relief of it almost calmed us for one sweet moment. We ran to the other stairwell. This one was smokey, but not nearly as bad, not nearly. And so down we went, all the way to the ground floor and out and down the street, two blocks, until we were sitting on a bench in a tiny New York City Park, dusk just falling around us.

Silence. Relief. And for me? Shame, shame, shame. The fresh, pointed stab of living in the moment that shame can bring. Everything else fades away, no more boredom, no more doubt, no more worrying about the future, the past, and Ron, just a drenching in self pity and the *now*. In that moment, everything was about me and my wrongness. It's a sort of baptism, when the floodgates of regret let loose.

"I'm sorry," I said. It was the right thing to say. For the first time, I noticed streaks of blood on my forearms; swollen and burning: cat scratches. The pain was a tonic for all my shame.

Lise sniffled and hugged her cat carrier. Dylan stared off into space. The stench of cat urine was comforting and mortal.

"I was scared," I said. And it was then that I realized she had finally seen me, me, *me*, her doormat friend. Her tacky friend. The one who walked too close to her, who didn't know what Crossroads or Sonic Youth was. I had finally made an impression on her. An ugly one, but an impression, nonetheless.

This was before I knew that we all live on this planet, driving in the cars of our own little minds, our own self-contained worlds. Yes, this was before I knew that, when I thought I mattered, when I thought that people saw me, deep into me, saw all my love and excitement at being alive, saw the very glistening, running-overness of my aliveness. But we only matter when we do something awful. Then, someone sees us and only then.

"Wow," said Dylan. "That was intense."

We were safe. Suddenly the sky darkened, like it does sometimes, and dusk was over. The lights in the tall buildings everywhere were pinpricks, little holes in the world, the holes of a safety net all around us. A time in my life was over and it had ended pretty badly. And yet, what a beautiful thing, to be young, to not yet even have discovered my own body (which hours under a bathtub spout eventually changed), to be at the mercy of others, to have so much ahead of myself, and to so easily disappoint another person.

· two years ·

HE WAS THE ONE TO GIVE HER HEAD WHEN SHE WAS ON THE RAG. He liked it, the saltiness, the nastiness of it. He grabbed her legs so hard it left bruises, because she claimed she didn't want him to go down on her when she was bleeding. Yeah, right. Her pussy was so clean anyway, even when she bled. The shock of it. He tongued her asshole, too. Fresh as a daisy, this girl. Broad daylight, on the lumpy futon on the floor of his room in an apartment in Allston, Mass. Totally naked, their skin pale and visibly human—veins, pimples—lit by the sun streaming in, the bright, midday sunlight. Some torn sheets hanging in the windows, not providing much protection from the fierce light. As they move, dust rises in the streams of light, surrounding their glowing bodies. It was noon, maybe 2 P.M. They'd been having sex all morning. Hungover sex, "hangover helper," he called it. She propped her head up on a pillow so she could watch his face in her cunt, the top of his forehead, his receding hairline, the dark, almost black strands of hair, his long, long hair, falling past his shoulders. Rock drummer hair. He'd look up at her. Pull his mouth away from her and she could see it, his mouth, dark where her blood streaked him. "I fucking love your pussy," he says quietly, a finger inside of her.

They didn't have much in common—he didn't read and she wasn't from the Boston area—but he changed her life the day he ate her out for an hour straight, moving the vibrator around inside of her, outside of her, and finally sticking a finger up her ass until she came. For the first time. A huge, huge blood curdling, screaming, flying across the room orgasm, that ended with her smacking her head against the wall. Did he levitate her? How'd she get so far off the ground, so high in the air? After that, he owned her. Not that he necessarily wanted to, but he did, and so that was that. And then she was terminally in his bedroom, naked, begging for it. *Please, Curt, please. Don't leave me. Don't don't.* Taking her clothes off, wanting him so badly, falling to her knees. Her hands gently petting his head, *God Curt, oh, oh,* moving his head ever so slightly, as he eats her out for the ten millionth time.

Actually, it wasn't always that way. At first he had to coax her. Come on, let me kiss you down there. She was barely nineteen and she'd blush. Oh don't do that. That's gross. Oh no it's not. And she'd let him do it and she'd get so excited and yell stop, stop and pull him up and into her. Which was fine. He'd fuck her and he liked doing that. She was ten years younger than him and skinny and—ten years younger than him. Pale nipples on her pointy little tits and a long perfect stomach with the tiniest little bulge resting in her narrow hips. Her pink, little girl cunt, with youth fluffing it up and dripping out of it. You're made for sex. You're built for this. Your pussy should be in magazines. He'd roll onto his back and sit her on top of him and lean her back, with her knees stretched as far apart as they could go, and instinctively (or maybe someone had told her, but he doubted it, because every other guy she'd fucked before him was some young, dumb college jock who'd fuck her doggy style with the lights off), gently, saying, yeah, yeah, with her left forefinger and middle finger, she'd pull herself wide open for him. Wide open in the middle of the day. He liked it. Liked seeing all that.

Later, they'd go shoot pool down the street. Or he'd be playing and the bass player would pick them up and drive them to the club. She'd watch him play drums. Standing directly in front of the stage with her friend Katie. The two in nearly matching Betsey Johnson skintight minidresses. Her mouth slightly open, shiny pale lip gloss, moving awkwardly to the music. She was a horrible dancer. And afterwards, she would come right up to him. Stand next to him, step on his foot. "Sorry," she says sheepishly, her brow anxiously furrowed. He just wanted to talk to his friends. And sometimes he had schmoozing to do—label people, a guitar player who may want to use him. His mother might be there. No matter, there'd Sonia be, right next to him. Her breath stinking of beer and cigarettes. She'd drink four beers during his set and smoke half a pack. Her arms folded nervously over her tiny chest. Her hair limp against her moonish face. Her mascara smeared. Okay, okay sometimes he'd be talking to a cute girl. No matter, Sonia wouldn't freak out. Her face stuck in this weird nervous position. He noticed then her double chin, from the way she held her head smooshed back into her neck. She wasn't fat, she was skinny, but she'd tense up and her chin would fold into itself. It was ugly. Her insecurity made her ugly. He hated her then.

But he'd drink four beers, and eventually Katie would drag Sonia away somehow, so Katie could talk to some guy, and he'd have fun talking to his friends. Smoke some weed. And then the bar would be closing—this was Boston, the bars closed at 2 A.M.—and he actually would want to bring her to Nat's house, some of the times. Sometimes, he didn't want to bring her. Sometimes, he just didn't want to deal with her, her being nervous and jealous. Other times, he wanted her warm body around, her cute, young, young body, her skinny legs sticking out of her tight minidress, wanted all that nervousness even, that he would pound out of her later. Pound pound pound her late at night, early in the morning, in the dark of his room, on the futon, sometimes as the sun came up. She was loud when he did it. And so it would start all over again. And as the sun trickled through the sheets in the windows, he could see her. Another day wasted in the lemon freshness of her youthful pussy, another day of playing with her young body and she bent over and under him with such desperation and abandon. Later, at four or so in the afternoon, he'd get her to buy him breakfast at the diner down the street. Then she'd go home to shower and change into another one of her slutty outfits—he didn't let her keep clothes at his house anymore. That he put an end to. He'd be listening to Neil Pert drum solos, playing air drums, and he'd hear the answering machine pick up, "Curt, Curt, are you there . . . ?"

Sonia, Sonia, go away! Why was it so hard to make her leave him? He treated her like shit—well, except for the fucking. He fucked her right. He couldn't help himself. A woman's body in his face and he had to do his job. It was enough for her, or so she claimed, but she was miserable. She'd given up all her self-respect, and for what? For his face between her legs. She was crazy. Sometimes, he blamed it all on her ass, but you can't base a relationship on an ass. Her flat, white, smooth-as-silk ass. Skin like a baby's. It killed him. A shapeless ass, small as a boy's. He loved her ass and loved opening her legs up underneath her ass. He didn't love her anymore—maybe he never did—but when she showed up at three in the morning, letting herself in with the keys he needed to take away from her, not turning on the lights, saying, I need you, I need you, slithering in bed with him, crying, breathing unevenly, uninvited, what could he do? Her mouth on his cock and he'd be hard in seconds and then it was too late. He had to get those keys from her. And tell her it was over.

He asked for the keys outside of the diner on Harvard Avenue one warm Spring afternoon. She'd just bought him French toast

with bacon, orange juice, and a cup of coffee. He asked her for
the keys, saying, this is not working, I need my space right now,
it's not you it's me, like that, on the street, so that she couldn't
start taking her clothes off. Or throw too much of a hysterical
fit, although she wasn't much into self-control. During that last
breakfast in the diner, she'd been weepy and whiny, we only see
each other twice a week, I mean, I guess it's okay, but why don't you
want to see me more? What's wrong with me? What don't you like
about me, sniffle, sniffle? I can change, I can, I really can.

No you can't. No one can. I can't either. He tries to tell her that
THAT is what he doesn't like about her, the what don't you like
about me, I can change. The sheer lack of pride. He can barely
look at her when she starts in with that pathetic shit. How could
he have let it go on for two years? Two years . . .

So what happens next? He already started fucking that girl in
Portland, the one with the nice Volvo. She stunk of money. And
she lived far away. Although he could see a future with her, her
money, her scowl, her no-bullshit attitude. The opposite of
Sonia's wimpiness. He needs a hard-headed woman, just like
Cat Stevens says. Meanwhile, lots of hang-ups on the machine.
Then a message from her. I need to talk to you. He doesn't call
back. More hang-ups. Then a week later, another message. And
then, a week after that, he picks up for some reason and it's her.
Just let me see you one more time. I need to talk to you. Okay,
he says, I'll drive over in the cab, I'm driving tonight.

· · ·

He drives over. It's dark, around 9 P.M. He honks. He's not parking. He's not going in there. The cab idles in front of the yellow house where she lives. He sees her come out the door and he steps out of his cab, leans against it. It makes him feel secure. She's lost weight, she's even skinnier than before. Her hair seems longer, stringier. She's wearing a tight miniskirt, like always. Those skinny legs look like he could break them with two fingers. She walks down the steps and onto the sidewalk. He folds his arms. He's not gonna let her make him feel guilty. He doesn't owe her anything, except 700 bucks. He doesn't owe her himself though, he doesn't owe her. He's afraid she's gonna fall down, she seems so weak, so pale, so helpless. Did he do this? It's her life, it's not his responsibility. Give me one more chance, she whispers, and he can barely hear her, the motor of the cab hums loudly. Did he read her lips? Please, give me one more chance, I can change, she croaks. One more, one more. But his arms remain folded, and he shakes his head, no. He gets in the cab and he sees out of the corner of his eye that she's walking back to the yellow house, and he's so relieved, he was afraid that she'd do something crazy, jump on the cab, throw herself at him, and he drives away, slowly at first, then faster, wishing he could go all the way to Portland tonight.

Ah, Sarah in Portland. Lies there like a board, but her pussy's as slick as a seal. When she comes, she makes the tiniest of noises, moves her hips one centimeter. Blip. And it's over. It's as if all that money keeps her mind off of her body. It's a relief. It's . . . low pressure. It feels like fucking a wife should. Sarah will be his wife, of this he feels sure. No more screaming and thrashing about. No more hysteria. No more Sonia! No more! Will he miss her? It seems impossible.

Curt pulls over to the cab stand on Harvard Avenue. A gaggle of BU girls walk down the street, swinging their glistening hair around in the clear New England night. They get in the cab in front of him and he pulls up to take its place. The night is young. Curt feels young. He turns on the radio and a Rush song is playing and he thinks, this is good, this is a good sign, and he takes his hands off the wheel, and with the utmost precision, air drums all of the fills.

• inside madeleine •

1

Her name was Madeleine. She ate French toast for breakfast. Or waffles or pancakes. Her mother's back to her, broad and strong, mixing the dough and frying the eggy bread until it was hot and golden brown. She stacked up a pile of five or six pieces and greased them slick with butter, careful to put butter on each piece, lifting the hot bread with her fingers, steam burning up from the stack. She poured on huge dollops of syrup, preferably a colorful blueberry or strawberry syrup, occasionally using brown maple syrup. If, for some strange reason, her mom didn't cook, then she ate three bowls of Captain Crunch or Boo Berrry or Count Chocula, letting the milk turn thick with the sugar and starch, drinking the milk down when there were no bites left. She spread raspberry jam on slices of toast already dripping with butter. Large chunks of jam, the seeds of the berries sticking between her teeth. She ate in a breathless stupor, staring at the cereal box or syrup bottle, reading the ingredients over and over to herself, her back hunched over the food protectively. Breakfast was her favorite. She often had trouble sleeping at night because hot, buttery pancakes raced through her head and the excitement she felt at the prospect of eating kept her up late into the night.

At lunchtime she came home to eat. Most kids ate cafeteria meals of microwaved meat and vegetables, a small carton of milk, and a piece of cake in the perfect-sized squares of the styrofoam trays. Other children ate sandwiches packed in brown bags with a chips and a Twinkie. But Maddy raced the two blocks home, and her mother's back would face her again, as she stirred pots of chicken soup with dumplings and fried potato pancakes with sour cream and applesauce. Maddy ate sausages cooked in the pan and split down the middle slathered with a mustard that brought tears to her eyes. She ate stews with meat and potatoes and carrots. Everything she ate she washed down with large glasses of milk, pushing down chunks of barely chewed food, food she swallowed so quickly her throat was often scratched. Then she ran back to school, her stomach as tight as a basketball, her belly pushing against the snap of her jeans. She ran the two blocks back so as not to miss the next class, the food hard and painful in her stomach.

After school she had a snack. Her mother's face would be in the paper, her feet up on a chair as she sat in the living room. Maddy would throw her books on the kitchen table and open the refrigerator and then open the cupboards. There was peanut butter on crackers and boxes of moist raisins. There were bags of pretzels and cheese wrapped in individual plastic slices. She ate fruit-flavored yogurts and candy bars and homemade cookies left in a tin. She ate slices of luncheon meats rolled up in a tube shape, her fingers holding on to the greasy meat, sliding it down the root of her tongue, swallowing it whole. She ate until she couldn't eat anymore and her stomach felt as tight as it did after lunch, stretched and hurting, and she'd lie down in the living room or on her bed, the blood flowing away from her mind, flowing straight to her stomach, leaving her sleepy and digesting.

She grew. She grew three and a half inches between the age of ten and eleven. Her shoe size went up two sizes. Her clothes bound her body uncomfortably. Her mother began standing behind her on the scale, watching the needle shake up and up as she continued to gain weight. Her mother took her shopping and bought her loose sweaters and shirts with matching elastic waist pants and new white underwear from the women's section of Goldblatt's department store. She wasn't allowed to wear prints, because they would draw attention to her girth. The matching outfits were in solid colors only, no whites or bright yellows, rather colors her mother thought were slimming, such as dark purple and dark blue. She bought a new winter coat and new fluffy, red mittens. She weighed well over two hundred pounds by the end of the sixth grade.

Her schoolmates called her Fatty, Fat Girl, Fatso, Jiggle Butt, Jelly Butt, Big Ass, Big Titties, Piggy, Cow, Lard Ass. They called her Maddy the Fatty, Moo Moo Maddy.

For dinner her mother cooked whole stuffed chickens and baked potatoes and steamed broccoli with hollandaise sauce.

Maddy ate beef Wellington and pork chops and baked fruit pies for dessert. There was cheese fondue and meatloaf and homemade pizzas with onions and sausage. They rarely went out to eat. Her mother's back, sturdy and industrious, preferred to stand guard at the counter in the kitchen. After dinner Maddy snacked while she watched TV. She ate donuts and bags of red licorice. She ate oatmeal cookie sandwiches that were filled with icing. Her stomach ached, stuffed hard, packed down with a shovel.

Her father stopped looking at her. He looked at the air next to her instead when he addressed her. Her mother cooked. Her sister Amanda was a teenager and didn't notice anything. Maddy ate and ate and ate. Her breasts grew but so did the rest of her body so they almost didn't seem like breasts, just an extension of the layers of fat and flesh that surrounded her. She grew hips that hid in the lumps of fat that accumulated above and below them. She grew pubic hair, strangely dark and prickly, under her arms and between her legs. Folds of peach-colored flesh hid the brown patches of fur. But they were there, dark and alarming, underneath all the layers.

Her hands grew big and round, dimpling in the palms. They perspired a thin wetness while pulling meat off of a chicken leg and grabbing handfuls of peanuts. Sweat came out of the pores in her chin and the many hidden folds of her flesh. Her armpits and inner thighs began smelling musty like a dirty drain in a bathtub. They stunk like brown hay, like a sink full of dirty pots. Her crotch smelled of lukewarm shrimp, salty and damp. The skin where her breasts met was covered with a film of mildewy sweat; her cleavage grew red and splotchy from the heat and damp and the rubbing against itself.

She bathed at night, filling the tub only halfway, sinking her huge body down and watching the water rise to the edges of the bath. She scrubbed herself with a washcloth, a bar of Ivory soap, rubbing herself until she turned pink and raw. She scrubbed her armpits and her breasts and feet and neck. She washed behind her ears and behind her knees. She rubbed the bar of soap between the lips of her crotch, sliding it down to the groove of her asshole. She rubbed it back and forth until her arms ached from reaching around her body and her crotch burned. And as soon as she stood up, the milky water now cool, dripping off her, she began to sweat again. As she vigorously rubbed a bath towel against her back and around her neck, her skin became damp again, her own fluids free to cover her body once more. By the time she lay down to sleep, she could smell herself strongly, smell a musty animal smell emanating from the secret parts of her ever expanding body.

Her schoolmates called her Stinky and Funky and Sweaty and PU and You Smell Like Shit. They plugged their noses with their hands when she maneuvered herself into her school desk. They called her Maddy the Fatty you smell like hell. They called her FatShitStink. She used prescription creme deodorant that came in a jar and a medicated body powder. Her mother washed her clothes separately from the rest of the family's with a scented detergent made for tough grease stains.

Her mother took her to a doctor. A specialist. A tall gray-haired man with a red, veiny face and bad breath. They drove two hours south of South Bend to see him. She undressed and put on a pale, flowered robe. He weighed her. He made her raise her arms. He made her try and touch her toes. He looked inside her mouth with a tongue depressor. He asked her why she ate so much. He felt her breasts and underneath her arms and asked her to breathe while he listened to her heart. She lay back on an examining table, and he prodded and asked and prodded some more. He gave her mother a strict diet for Maddy to follow and a prescription medicine to reduce appetite. He asked her if she would like them to put a ball in her stomach. He said this sternly, his eyes hooded by dark drooping lids. He said, with a clammy hand on her bare shoulder, that it would be a serious operation. For six months the ball would remain inside of her, he said, sewn up into her gut so that she would fill up easily and not eat much at all. They drove home and looking at the road ahead, her mother cried. The operation would be expensive.

Every morning and every night she stepped on the scale and her mother stood behind her and watched the needle dance. Every morning and every night she took two red prescription capsules that left her head jittery and hollow. She ate dry toast for breakfast and drank a diet chocolate shake that came in a can. She came home for lunch and was given a bowl of fruit. She drank glasses and glasses of water with squeezed lemon. Endless ice cubes rattled against her teeth. She ate specially prepared chicken for dinner, grilled with herbs and served with white rice. She had a pink book with the words *My Little Food Book* on it where her mother wrote down everything she ate and how many calories it contained. Her mother bought her exercise clothes and new sneakers. Sweat suits and rubber sweat clothes. Maddy jumped rope in the kitchen while her mother cooked, counting the turns of the rope out loud, twenty-three, twenty-four, twenty-five. She ran around their neighborhood block five times with her mother every night. The neighbors looked out of their windows at first. Small, featureless faces peering sideways out windows. Parents and children walking from their cars to their front doors, stopping momentarily, necks turning to watch the woman pull her daughter down the block. Sweat poured out of Maddy faster than before, more watery than ever, staining her bright athletic clothes with dark, damp patches.

At night she dreamt of the breakfast of her past, she dreamt the hot sweet odor of pancakes and bowls of sticky cereal. She dreamt dishes of delicious food were in front of her and her hands were larger than ever; so thick were her fingers that they could not hold onto a spoon or a fork. As she tried to grasp them, the utensils would fall out of her useless swollen hands, clanging to the floor. She dreamt of thick stews and double hamburgers. Sometimes in her dreams she could eat and she would. In these dreams she ate and ate and ate, and when she woke, her stomach burned with acidic juices cruelly aroused for no real purpose.

She menstruated deep, brown blood that flowed for ten days straight. Soon after that her mother drove her to see the special doctor again. He weighed her, wrapped up in the same flowered robe. He made her touch her toes and reach for the ceiling, and he poked his clammy finger under her arms and in the small of her back. He looked at the inside of her mouth. He asked her how she felt, his brow wrinkled, his malodorous breath in her face. She told him fine.

But she felt like a deflated balloon, a neglected doll, a stuffed animal attacked by a dog. She felt small and see-through, less protected, less herself. She had been MaddyFatty, StinkyCow, Pigface. She had been Jiggly Jelly Butt. She had been round and soft, her eyes hidden behind folds, the shape of her chin and nose lost behind flesh.

But now all of her came out in sharp relief. She looked at herself in the mirror in the doctor's office, wrapped up in the flowered robe. Her breasts had become their own shapes, separate from the rest of her body, large tuberous things, protruding outward from her newly slimmer waist. Her hips flared out like fans, swinging side to side as she walked. Her eyes came out, big and visible to the world, wet and round and white. Her nose became thin and angled and her chin pointed outward, a lonely exposed bone. She had lost sixty pounds and lost her names, her flesh pillows, her body as she knew it. Her mother beamed as she stared at the road in front of her on the drive home, her eyes shining glossy and her mouth curled with joy. No ball would be surgically implanted in her daughter's stomach. No more expensive doctor visits. Maddy would just stick to her routine. Everything would be fine.

2

When Madeleine turned twelve she was five nine and a hundred and seventy pounds. That September she started the seventh grade and she felt nervous, fat, and ashamed. She worried about the clothes she wore to the extent that she didn't sleep well at night and her breath came short and fast in the mornings, or sometimes all day, depending on what she was wearing. Lunch time was the hardest because she no longer could run home, the junior high was too far away, so she had to eat at the cafeteria. After a few humiliating days of eating alone, she sat at a table with a handful of girls that looked around at each other with irritated and vulnerable eyes. It was a table that soon disappeared altogether, the girls sitting together only so as not to be alone, and as quickly as possible, they migrated to real, defined groups—the preps, the jocks or the nerds. Madeleine knew some of the preppie kids from her elementary school but her view of them changed drastically in the first few weeks of seventh grade (she had once thought them important) and eventually they fell from her vision altogether, becoming vague, uninteresting phantoms that roamed the school in Izod shirts and cableknit sweaters. Instead, she found herself mysteriously drawn to the freaks, and without realizing it, she began following them around, especially a small, wiry girl named Jennifer.

The freaks, of which Jennifer was a kind of queen, were generally from the south side of South Bend, and the boys had long, stringy hair and wore heavy metal T-shirts; their shoulders were slumped and they didn't look people in the eye. The girls dressed in tight, revealing clothing bought at discount stores, wore too much make-up and had bleached, feathered hair with dark roots showing. Both the girls and the boys had the reputation of being violent and mean and were rumored to carry knives with them. And although they were not thought of as stupid, they were known to get bad grades, because they didn't care, because they smoked pot, because they were troubled. Maybe it was from fear, or curiosity or a kind of respect, maybe it was some knowledge they seemed to have, but Madeleine was drawn to their lunch table and their ways, her voice became twanged and filled with "ain'ts" and her look became less respectable. Mostly, she wanted to be Jennifer.

Jennifer was perfect. She was thin and petite, her eyes were hard and she always was impeccably dressed. Her sweaters outlined her smallish, well defined breasts perfectly and her pants were tight and new looking, without a pantyline to mar the boyish curve of her bottom. Her piercing laugh was distinctly cruel and always directed at someone. But otherwise she spoke deep and low; and other kids would have to lean toward her to hear her, which they did nervously. She often slapped people on the arm or shoulder, biting her thin bottom lip as she did, and it hurt, stung for minutes, but it was just play and no one could get angry about it.

Madeleine simply became Jennifer's shadow. She did this discreetly, unknowingly on anyone's part at first, especially her own. When Jennifer laughed, she laughed. When Jennifer kicked gravel, Madeleine did. She smoked Marlboro Lights because Jennifer did. Jennifer lined her dark eyes heavily with a Maybelline eyeliner and her cheeks sparkled with blush that came out of a pink plastic case. Madeleine began darkening her eyelids with the same brand of eyeliner and stroked her robust cheeks with the same sparkly powder. She wore the same boots as Jennifer; brown with thick red laces. And Madeleine began swearing frequently with a violent enthusiasm, her sentences littered with fucks and shits, as if it were a part of her she had kept hidden all her childhood and finally set free. When Jennifer craned her neck around to look at something, Madeleine's plump neck carefully followed in the same direction, a peripheral eye ever on her friend, in case she were to change the course of her gaze.

She called Jennifer every day after school. When they spoke, Jennifer spoke of all the boys she knew, who was going out with whom, which girls did what with which boys, and Madeleine listened hungrily, curled up in the back of her parent's closet so nobody could hear her, the phone held tensely on her lap, surrounded by her mother's shoes.

Yeah, Marion is a slut. Last year she fucked half of the senior class at the high school. She thinks no one remembers because they've all graduated. But a slut's a slut, said Jennifer.

Yeah, and I can't believe she fucked that guy in his car, said Maddy.

What do mean you can't believe it?

I just can't believe it. How gross. Where were they?

I just said for the millionth time, they were in his car.

I mean, where was the car. Were they parked?

No, dumbshit, they were driving around while they fucked. What's your problem? Of course they were parked. You can't fuck someone when you're driving around. You're such a virgin.

Fuck you, I am not.

Yes you are. A fat virgin.

Fuck you.

Fuck you, Jennifer mimicked.

I am not a virgin.

Okay then. Who have you fucked?

I fucked Tim Spencer last year, lied Madeleine.

The previous year, while playing five minutes in the closet, Tim, a nervous, skinny boy with protruding front teeth that obviously bothered him, had groped at her breasts and put a twitching hand between her legs on the outside of her jeans.

No way. Tim Spencer couldn't fuck no one if he tried. No way in hell. That nerd doesn't have a dick.

Fuck you. You're a bitch.

I gotta go.

Okay, I'll see you tomorrow.

Bye.

After they talked, Madeleine would sit in the closet for a while, her heart beating fast, her lips moist, her mouth full of saliva. She'd stay there until her mother would come to the closet door, yelling, asking her what on earth she was doing, and Madeleine caring little about her mother's frustration, stumbled out and into her own room and planned out what she would wear the next day. She fingered her clothes, spreading pants and sweaters out on the bed; she'd look at an outfit and change her mind, deciding on another sweater. Meanwhile, images of Marion fucking someone in a car raced through her head. And as she lay in bed, curled up in a big, cozy ball, with a warm hand between her thighs, she thought of Jennifer; of the way Jennifer held her body tight and erect, with her shoulders slumped slightly and self-consciously, of the way Jennifer walked down the halls, her bowed, short legs gliding quickly, her feet hitting the shiny, hard tiles and clicking solidly.

Now at lunch time, Madeleine without question joined Jennifer at a table in the back of the cafeteria. It was known as the freak table. The table differed from the other tables in that it never lined up in quite the same direction as the rest, rather it pointed in a strange angle, and the lunch trays were extraordinary in their sloppiness. Food was left uneaten and graying, feet were propped up on the table despite this being against the rules. Bags of pot and switchblades and dirty magazines were passed from one dirty fingernailed hand to another. Everyone who sat there owned a blue jean jacket, preferably an old beat up one, and all of the boys wore their blue jean jackets year round—even in the worst months of winter. After they finished poking at their lunch, the crowd gathered around by a side entrance of the school and smoked joints and cigarettes. Conversation and eye contact were spare— lots of gravel was kicked. Madeleine never spoke at all, but by the time she entered her next class, she felt powerful and dangerous. She was aware of her growing reputation.

Madeleine's parents began noticing the change in her, which her father tried to ignore and her mother occasionally yelled and cried over. Madeleine became unrecognizable to her family, her hair burnt and twisted from the curling iron, her face orange with cheap make-up, leaving a trail of Coty musk perfume behind her as she awkwardly roamed the malls, fast food restaurants and skating rinks of South Bend, two steps behind Jennifer wherever they were. They shopped together at the discount stores, buying the same outfits in different shades—Jennifer's in purple, Madeleine's in pink. They took Polaroids of each other and had people photograph them together when they were at the mall, leaning against each other in their matching outfits, their arms folded against their chests, one foot crossed arrogantly over the other.

The two girls usually spent the weekends at Jennifer's house, side by side in the bathroom, applying and reapplying eye shadows. On Friday nights, they skated at Howard's Park ice rink. The two rink guards who worked there, Scott and Oz, were in their last years of high school after having repeated a few years. They drove loud cars that had red stripes painted on the sides and they spoke with deep weathered voices. Jennifer talked with Scott and Madeleine talked with Oz by default, he being the less attractive one. Madeleine followed Oz around the rink just enough to annoy him rather than amuse him, laughing at inappropriate moments, staring at him, slack-jawed. She was somewhat aware of her effect on him and she continued to pursue him with the belief that next time, she'd say the right thing. And on occasions, Oz would look upon her with some sign of interest, or something that appeared to be interest, and Madeleine would get dizzy and skate away, covering her broad, uncontrollable smile with large, mittened hands. Every hour on the hour the Zamboni would smooth the ice and the two girls would convene in the bathroom, their tarted-up faces red from the cold, and comb their hair with combs they kept in their back pockets.

I think he likes me, said Madeleine.

I think he likes me, mimicked Jennifer, her voice high and nasal.

Stop it, you bitch. I think he does.

Jennifer continued primping in the mirror, tucking her tight, fluffy acrylic sweater into her jeans and then she slapped Madeleine on the shoulder.

I think he does, Jennifer squawked.

Madeleine ignored her taunting for a moment and assuredly stated: I'm going to lie to him and tell him I'm fifteen.

I'm gonna lie to him and tell him I'm fifteen.

Stop it!

Stop it!

Madeleine didn't tell Oz she was fifteen that night, but she skated around slowly, her hands deep in the pockets of her turquoise ski jacket, planning the perfect way of telling him, how she would toss her hair, how he would smile at her. That night, like most Friday nights Madeleine and Jennifer slept together

on Jennifer's narrow mattress, their skin damp and swollen
with sleep, their bodies tired from skating. Madeleine had
trouble sleeping. She lay quietly next to her friend, imitat-
ing the way her breath came and left, the way her stomach
rose and fell, aware of herself and Jennifer's body next to
her. She woke up that Saturday morning and her arms and legs
ached and she was quieter than usual as she and Jennifer ate
their cereal together.

The next weekend they went skating again and Madeleine
wore a brand new pink velour V-neck sweater that made her
self-conscious of her large breasts. It was tight and shiny and
her cleavage was prominently displayed. Before they left Jennifer's house, Madeleine stood in front of the full-length mirror
in the bathroom and practiced saying, I'm fifteen, and, I bet you
didn't know I was fifteen, and she put her hands on her hips
and then on her thighs, tilting her hips this way or that, and she
smiled at her reflection with her head turned downward, looking up at herself coyly. She sprayed an extra squirt of Coty musk
perfume on her neck, telling herself that it was for good luck. It
was a particularly cold November evening and she skated up to
Oz soon after they got there.

Hey Oz, she said, reaching out awkwardly to grab the sleeve
of his leather jacket.

What?

I'm fifteen.

No you're not.

Oh yes I am. I swear it.

Then how come I've never seen you at the high school. Huh?

I don't know, Madeleine said, looking down at her skates and touching her toes together, the blades scraping against each other.

You're not from this part of town, are you, he said, looking straight at her and it unsettled her but she was flattered. He had never spoken so many words to her before.

I *am* fifteen.

He laughed, saying, Well, you're tall enough. He wet his lips and appeared as if he had decided on something.

I am. I was born in 1965. That makes me fifteen.

Well, if you say so sweetie. That still makes you a lot younger than me, almost five years younger. Now what do you think of that?

I think that's just fine.

Madeleine smiled broadly, unable to refrain from doing so and she lifted her colorful, wool knit mittens to her face.

You think that's just fine!

He laughed, throwing his head back, his mouth open wide, revealing more fillings than she'd ever seen.

Well my little fifteen-year-old girl, it looks like it's time to get off the rink. It looks like it's time for the Zamboni to clean off the ice, he said and then paused a beat, and looking away from her, added: Why don't you come with me. He skated around in a small circle and she couldn't catch his eye.

Come with you? Where to? Maddy asked. She put her toes together and then slid her heals together, toes then heals, without looking at her skates.

To the rink guard's station, where else? Where did you think I meant?

Oz brushed his hair away with black, dirty leather gloves and revealed a small forehead and tired, gray eyes and for a moment she was alarmed.

I don't know. How was I supposed to know.

Her cheeks felt puffy, like baby's cheeks, and her face was hot with blood that had rushed to it.

Let's go.

He skated over to the rink guard's station, with its PRIVATE sign on the door.

Fifteen-year-old girls aren't as shy as you, he said. Then he snickered, quiet and light, and she looked at his teeth. They were tobacco-stained and too small for his head. Her ankles wobbled as she followed him.

I'm coming.

He held on to the sleeve of her ski jacket, coaxing her firmly yet softly into the room, and it occurred to Madeleine that no one had ever been that gentle with her before. A fluorescent light hung from the ceiling, giving everything a hard, green appearance. There was a bench and a desk with a chair, a girlie calendar on the wall, and overflowing ashtrays everywhere. Oz lit a joint, sat on the bench, and pulled her next to him. He grinned, the light making his face veiny and green. She smoked, aware of his hockey skates, and she noticed that his feet were actually larger than hers.

You have big feet, she said.

You've got big eyes, he said, laughing quietly, nicely and added, They're pretty. I like them.

He grinned and his grin seemed permanent, endless, and she tried not to stare at his teeth.

Come here, he said, I want to touch you. That's a girl.

She scooted closer to him, their bodies were touching and his arm was heavy around her shoulder. His arm felt protective and affectionate, and she liked it, but the inside of her mouth was swollen and dry, making her uncomfortable. He leaned into her face, kissing her ear and she sensed a tension in his body.

Relax, he whispered hoarsely, but his body was far from relaxed, it was tight and rigid and he kissed her ear again and Madeleine's heart slammed against her breasts as she looked down shamefully on the whiteness of her swelling cleavage. Oz ran his hands over her neck and his fingers were slightly damp and cold. Oh baby, he murmured, biting his lip, just relax, that's it, I won't hurt you.

She leaned her head back and closed her eyes, her muscles twitched under her skin; she felt each one jerk, her shoulder, her stomach, her thigh. Oz reached toward the zipper of her jeans and she opened her eyes and put her hand out halfheartedly to stop him and he gently put her hand away. He undid her jeans and quickly slipped a clammy hand into her underwear, saying, that's it. You like this don't you?

Madeleine tilted her hips upward, letting her thighs spread to accommodate his hand. A warmth ran through her body and suddenly the light hurt her eyes so she shut them again.

You're wet, baby. God you're wet, he said, grinning, and she opened her eyes and looked straight into his mouth, straight at his teeth. Then his hand was in front of her face, glistening and mossy smelling. Look at how wet you are, he said and touched her lips with his damp hand. He put his fingers back inside of her and she felt them hard this time, scraping against her soft, swollen flesh.

Ouch, that hurts, she said and Oz grinned, removing his fingers.

I want to fuck you. Okay?

He stood, pulling down his tight pants. He put out his hand and she reached up and held on to it, careful to look at his face, at his tired eyes, and he pulled her up off the bench. Then he pulled down her jeans and underwear and she twisted and squirmed to help him along. He pulled them down around her ankles, like his were, and he sat down, pulling her on his lap, with her back facing him, his long fingers gripping her already broad hip bones, sliding himself into her.

That feels good doesn't it, he said, you are a big girl aren't you, a big, big girl.

He moved her then with his strong, gripping hands, back and forth, then up and down, then back and forth again.

You're as big as a woman, big there where I'm in you, big as a woman who's had three kids, he said laughing and though she couldn't see him, she knew his head was thrown back and she saw his fillings and his awful brown teeth. Madeleine smelled herself in the room, the whole room smelled of her, and she wondered why it didn't hurt like it was supposed to, like it had when his fingers were inside of her, like Jennifer said it had, and she thought about how she'd tell Jennifer all about it at night, laying next to her on the thin mattress.

After a few moments, Oz gripped her hard and groaned a little. Then, with one hand on her head, he moved her off of his lap. They pulled up their pants in silence and she looked at him; he seemed anxious. Shit, he muttered, I gotta get out there.

As they walked out onto the ice rink, he calmly skated away, toward the other rink guard. Madeleine saw Jennifer come out of the bathroom and she glided quickly over to her friend, her mittens up to her face, covering a nervous, painful grin. Her breath came out moist and floated like damp smoke in the cold air and she put her arms around Jennifer's neck, saying, Oh God Jennifer—Fucking shit. You're not going to believe this, and Jennifer ducked her head and twisted herself away from Madeleine's grip.

Get off me, man, Jennifer said, and her arms flew out sharply from her compact frame. Madeleine winced.

Where the fuck were you, Jennifer snapped, her mouth tight.

I was in the rink guard's station.

Madeleine's words echoed in her head. She breathed out wetly again, her breath visible against the black air. The darkness of the sky had come down in front of her like a wall of water.

You were where?

I was in the rink guard's station. With Oz.

Jesus fucking Christ. You whore.

Jennifer spat on the ice. She turned around and skated back toward the bathroom. Madeleine watched her skate away—watched her enter the bathroom. Then she faced her large head to the sky, the sky that had darkened to a crisp black, the sky that surrounded her. Her groin ached, throbbing like a heartbeat, and holding her crotch with her mittened hands, she counted the throbbing beats, one, two, three.

3

From that day on she felt inside herself with fascination. The lights off, the house asleep, she lay on her back, her legs spread eagle, groping underneath her pink, flannel nightie, past her round belly into herself. She put a finger and then two inside. She turned herself over, squatting on her knees, quietly, hunched up underneath her covers, her head and shoulders pressing against her pillow. She put two then three then four fingers inside. Afterward, in those moments before sleep takes over, her breath slowing down and steadying, she put her fingers to her face and smelled her earthy smell and licked her hand. I'm big, she thought. I'm big like a woman who's had three children.

When she bathed, she practiced more. The water lubricating her, in went one finger then two then three. Soon her hand slid deftly in. She then put bars of soap and within weeks, shampoo bottles inside of herself. Up went her rubber ducky. Up went the washcloth. Her mother would knock impatiently on the door, saying, Maddy, get out of there, you'll shrivel up like a prune. She left the bathroom damp and cold, water splashed on the floor, wet towels everywhere. How can you make such a mess, her mother asked. Madeleine ignored her, huffed and shut the door to her bedroom. She'd lie in bed, her skin dry and tight, her body cleaned and stretched. She pulled her pubic hairs up, tugging the still damp strands, twisting the course hair around her fingers, until with a quick burning sting, they came out.

She got infections. Ingrown pubic hairs. Yeast infections. Bladder infections. Pelvic inflammatory disease. Her mother took her to a gynecologist, sniffling, asking, what's wrong with my girl? Are you having sex, Maddy, oh God, be careful. The doctor, a youngish man with an eye twitch asked, are you currently having sexual intercourse with anyone? She lay propped up on a table her feet in stirrups as he put in a speculum and said just relax, oh that's great, and she thought yeah, you think that's relaxed, you should see what I can fit up there and she closed her eyes as he prodded around inside of her and she imagined sucking him up there, where she had had the rubber ducky last night. She said I'm not having sex with anyone. He mother drove her home, sniffling. Maddy sat with her arms crossed across her chest, her thick bottom lip sticking out. She'd look out the car window and count the trees passing by. The doctor fit her with a diaphragm that she never used except sometimes late at night, by herself, pushing it in and out of herself before placing the saucer back into its plastic container. She put it in her drawer by her bed—but she knew her mother checked on it while she was at school, checked to see if the spermicidal jelly had been used.

She woke in the mornings tired, dark rings under her eyes, her fingers smelling that mossy smell. Her insides would be tender at times and she carried this tender feeling around with her at school like a secret trophy. In classes, she'd look at certain boys, boys who once seemed intimidating and powerful and she'd smile at them knowingly, thinking, I could put you inside of me, I could eat you up.

Once, when her parents had returned to bed early and she sat up with her older sister Amanda watching TV, she asked her how big she thought she was there.

What?

You know, down there. How big are you?

You're disgusting, Maddy.

Just tell me.

I don't know.

Can you put a finger up there?

Of course I can. I can put a tampon up there.

Can you put all your fingers up there?

I wouldn't know. Honestly, you are sick.

Shortly thereafter, her mother approached her bedside. Nervously, she discussed the facts of life with her daughter, explaining how the size of one's vagina changes to accommodate different things. A man's penis. A baby. Her dark eyes darted around the room. She wiped a greasy strand of hair from her forehead. She coughed and kissed her daughter goodnight on the forehead, her lips hard and tight.

Jennifer no longer talked to Maddy. Maddy's new best friend was an equally small girl with dull, tan eyes and an extensive knowledge of sexual things. Her name was Carrie and she had had sex with many high school boys. Carrie was in Madeleine's math class and they often did homework together, which meant Maddy let her copy her homework.

How big are you down there? Maddy asked her one day.

Big enough.

Big enough for what?

For dick, silly. For big dick.

I think I'm bigger than most.

Oh yeah? Well, you're a big girl.

Yeah, but even for a big girl.

At Carrie's house, Maddy convinced her friend to show herself. Carrie's mother was spending the night at her boyfriend's house and the two girls had smoked a joint and were watching TV.

Come on. Let me see. I want to see what yours looks like.

You're a pervert, Carrie said, her eyes narrowing, but she appeared intrigued.

Come on, Carrie. I'll show you mine.

Carrie stood up and pulled down her jeans.

Promise not to tell anyone we did this? I don't want people thinking we're lesbos or anything.

Yeah. Of course. I won't tell.

She wore striped blue panties that were delicately stained yellow in the crotch. She pulled them down and kicked them off. She stood there, revealing a tan-colored patch of hair between her thin legs and nothing else.

See, she said.

I want to see the inside, Maddy said.

Carrie blushed and frowned. The TV illuminated her from behind and she sat down and spread her legs.

There.

Maddy looked. She saw two, small pink mounds. She was disappointed.

Let me spread it open.

Carrie didn't say anything and Madeleine with one hand, gently opened up the pink flesh. Nothing there, she again was disappointed. She wanted to see a dark hole, an endless, vast tunnel.

How big of dick have you put in there?

I don't know.

Carrie got up and dressed.

Show me.

Carrie distanced her hands in front of her face. Like this big, she said and shrugged, like ten inches. Fat ones, too.

Madeleine leaned back on a cushion and looked toward the TV and said, do you want to see mine?

Sure. Why not.

Maddy removed her pants and sat like her friend had, with

her legs spread apart. With one large hand she pulled herself wide open and looked up at Carrie, who squinted between her legs.

Ugh. That's disgusting.

It's big, isn't it?

I don't know. It's gross, though. All pussy is gross.

What do you mean you don't know? It's big!

I guess so. It's just gross.

Carrie looked at the TV.

Maddy buttoned up her clothes. The next night, at her own house, she took her father's shaving mirror out of the bathroom and locking her door, peered at her insides in the mirror. Carrie was right. From the outside its capacity wasn't entirely visible, but she was not so easily deceived. She put three fingers inside and then looked. Yes, indeed, she thought. Yes I do.

She began stealing vegetables from the fridge. Cucumbers, carrots, whole bunches of celery. Her mother thought she was eating them and occasionally said something to her daughter. When did you eat all of those, she'd say, looking at Maddy with narrow, suspicious eyes. Well at least it's just vegetables, she'd say to her daughter. And Maddy did eat them—but only after she put them inside her. She shopped with her mother, buying the large, economy-sized bottles of shampoo. During her nightly bath, she worked up to putting them inside of her. Her crotch was smooth, baby peach, from pulling at all the pubic hairs. She wanted the whole world in there, she wanted the whole world to disappear in her cunt so that she could slide it—gleaming, coated damp—back out again. By the end of the seventh grade, she decided to do so.

4

She fucked the rink guard Oz again and the other one that Jennifer was never going to fuck. She fucked friends of theirs, too. On Friday nights, her mother would drop her and her new friend Carrie off at the rink. Sometimes Jennifer would be there but she never said hi to Carrie and Madeleine. Oz told his friends about her and they drove to Howard Park to see her, their souped-up cars roaring. She imagined the things he said to them. She's beautiful. She has beautiful breasts. She'll make you come so hard. With her mouth. With her cunt. She's the best there is. And she'd think about their cocks, all big and hard, just for her. She made them that rigid, that sleek. They lost control for her. She drove them wild.

But it wasn't quite like that and Maddy knew it. She knew they came to see her, but she also knew the things Oz said to them were different than she imagined.

They came in carloads of two up front and two in the back. Cute, tall, short, pimply, mean, quiet, scared, rough. Big cocks, small ones, but they were always hard. Pressed up against tight jeans. They'd get hard before she got in the car. They'd get hard just leaning over the rail of the ice rink, as Carrie and Maddy skated up to them in hot pink ski jackets that matched their hot pink lips. Their eyes sticky with sparkly blue eyeshadow and thick, thick mascara.

They'd get hard as they asked the girls to come out and drive around, shifting from leg to leg, tight blue jeans revealing it, hands in their pockets, nervously looking around. Carrie would work the front and Maddy would work the back because they fit better that way. But it changed, too. Depending on who the boys wanted. Some dark skinned Italian boy who sat behind the wheel, compact and gruff, saying, come here Mad girl, come here. Get your big ass up here I don't want that little skinny girl, his eyes black and round. And Maddy would smile smile smile, so wanted, so so wanted, and she'd get up front with him and Carrie would jump in the back.

Their cocks hard against their jeans, thick, lumplike. She put her hand on it. Looking at it in their pants. Looking at the boy looking at his own thing, looking at her hand on his cock still nestled in his jeans. She unzipped their jeans, carefully, so as not to hurt the goods, some zippers moved right along, other stuck and rusted, took a while. Those were the best. The boys' mouths would open, they'd get anxious, breathless, they'd put their hands there to help, sometimes grabbing the zipper from her and undoing it themselves, sometimes pulling out their hard cocks, sometimes leaving it in their Jockey underwear for her to pull out. They wanted it so bad it hurt them. Their cocks bouncing up, straining in their own skins. Beads of sticky clearness on top, quivering, dripping. So ready to blow Maddy bit her lip, trying not to laugh.

She put her hand on it. Stroked it gently stroked it hard. She put her mouth on it, licking it. Jesus, girl. Oh my God. Grunt. Moan. She put it all the way back in her big lipsticky mouth. Tight hands in her hair, sweating palms. It never took long. They were powerless. Sometimes they pulled her up and put it in her, pulling her jeans down over her round ass, sticking it straight in without a finger to her cunt. Just pushing it right in there and sliding it in like butter because she was always wet and she was always ready.

She fucked all the rink guards' friends. Joey, John, Matt, Bobby. All the high school freaks. Long-haired, combs in back pockets, pot in the glove compartment, AC/DC, Black Sabbath on the radio. She fucked them so good, fucked them better than the high school girls—fuckmonster Maddy, only a little junior high student. They told the other high schoolers. They told the football team, they told the basketball players, they told all the boys who needed to fuck.

She walked around her junior high, her head in the clouds, her thoughts on the weekends. The boys her age were small, lifeless things. Skinny, nervous, looking at her large, proud chest, hands in their pockets, playing with themselves. Sometimes, the ballsy ones, would say, hey Maddy I hear you give good head. She'd look straight at them, some younger brother of some boy she fucked, and they'd run away laughing, turning their heads back to look at her as they ran away, laughing at her. Pussies, she'd sneer. Little fucking momma's boys. No one's ever touched your little cock. If you have one. Sometimes they'd come back, chins up, moist upper lip, saying, oh yeah. You want to see my cock? Their hands in their pants. She'd say, whip it out then why dontcha. Little faggot boy. Your fucking baby cock, I'll laugh right at it. And they're in their pants now groping around all nervous too scared to whip it out. And they say you whore, you fucking whore, pants unzipped, hand on their hard neglected little cock, too scared to show it and she'd say your mother's a whore boy, that's why you were born.

When she graduated from junior high most of the high school boys she fucked had graduated from the high school. So she roamed the halls of the new, bigger school, coolly, mostly anonymous. The boys sometimes still came by the rink looking for her. Their cars bright red, engines loud as shit. But she grew tired of them, she started to see the lines on their foreheads and the pathetic look in their eyes. No longer in high school they moved out of their homes. Some moved in with their girlfriends and got married and stopped coming by now that they had pussy waiting for them at home. They had stupid jobs at garage stations and plants and factories and record stores. Their eyes grew duller and their brows wrinkly so she thought, no more of these old guys. The ones who didn't marry moved in with each other, Tim and Steve and whoever and their apartments stunk of rotten garbage and stale beer in the filthy carpeting. Sitting around on beat-up couches and La-Z-Boys, their heads hanging low, turtlelike, crunched over, sitting around watching the same TV shows. They'd call her on the phone, saying Maddy why don't you come over here and she did a few times but she liked them better when they were in high school. They had more confidence then.

So she walked around that high school with a shadow about her but hardly anyone there was anyone she'd fucked. People looked at her, curious, having heard some thing or another, but they hadn't experienced her. She picked and chose. She wore red high heels and tight jeans and backcombed her hair. She scared them all. She chewed gum loudly in class, she got great grades and she knew she could fuck whoever she wanted and knew she'd fuck them better than they'd ever been fucked before. So she fucked the ones she chose to fuck. She fucked the ones who deserved her shit. And then she fucked Mark.

5

He smiled at her in the hallway. His lips together, looking straight into her eyes, which very few people did. Most everyone looked at her sideways, including her teachers. Then he walked up to her while she was at her locker, so quietly she didn't hear him and tapped her on the shoulder. He was taller than he appeared, narrow and slightly slouched. He asked her if she wanted to get coffee after school and she smiled at him wryly. Why wasn't he fidgeting? Why wasn't he looking away, embarrassed? She said no and laughed in his face, but she watched him walk away, noticing his long limbs and his loping gate.

A week later he came up to her again.

Well, look who's here again, she said sarcastically.

You should have coffee with me.

I don't drink coffee.

You can order something else.

Coffee doesn't get me in the mood.

He looked down at her breasts, tightly encased in an AC/DC T-shirt. He looked up at her and smiled.

I'll buy you a beer, then.

Oooh, think you can handle that, she said and cocked her hips out.

Sure. I'll pick you up here after classes, he said, pushing his hands in his pockets.

Madeleine shut her locker, saying, sure thing, big boy.

He waved to her like a child as he sauntered off down the crowded hallway.

After school, Maddy packed her books and started off to the side entrance. Mark came running after her.

Hey, wait up. You said I could buy you a beer.

Don't believe everything you hear.

Ah, come on. Let me buy you a beer. Please.

He put his hand on her shoulder and gripped it tightly.

Get your fucking hand off me.

Okay, okay Mark said, waving his hands in surrender, I'm sorry.

What kind of beer are you going to buy?

Any kind you want.

Do you have any weed?

Sure. I've got great weed.

You've got great weed? I find that hard to believe.

I've got the best weed. California Sensemilia.

No shit? I'm there, she said, pulling him toward the exit, I want to see this great weed.

The weed *was* great. He pulled a plastic bag of light green, red-haired, sticky buds out of the glove compartment of his Chevy Nova. They both sat in the front seat and locked the doors and cracked their windows open. Madeleine was impressed.

I didn't know smart guys like you smoked killer pot.

What do you mean?

You hang out in the computer room all the time. I didn't know you computer nerds smoked weed.

We smoke the best weed there is. All your freak friends smoke shitty stuff.

Fuck you man, they smoke good stuff.

Mark expertly rolled a tight joint, licking the paper with flicks of his tongue.

Bullshit. They smoke homegrown, leafy stuff that gives you a headache.

How do you fucking know what they smoke?

I've gotten stoned with them before. With that crowd.

She laughed at him, saying, I doubt that.

I have.

He lit the joint and took a huge drag and passed it to her.

They'd kick your ass before they'd let you get stoned with them.

Not true, he said, his voice muffled from holding in the pot smoke. The car filled up with a sweet, strong odor as he slowly exhaled. He smiled and coughed a little and said, you're just too busy giving head so you don't notice anything.

I keep my eyes open when I give head. I notice everything.

Well, I've gotten stoned with your stupid freak friends and their pot sucks, he said, smiling confidently at her, and you've never noticed that.

The pot made them giggly. Madeleine felt especially giggly because she was with a nerd. His hair was short and he wore brown loafers. They drove to a liquor store and Mark went in and bought a six pack of Budweiser. They drove to Howard Park and sat parked facing the St. Joe River, drinking beer. She worried that they would run into someone she knew and she didn't want to be seen with him. After they finished the six pack, she put her hand on his crotch. He wasn't hard.

Stop that.

Why?

She grabbed harder.

Seriously, stop that.

Oooh, you're shy, she laughed, no one's ever touched you before.

That's not true.

Then why are you scared, stud boy?

I'm not scared.

Why can't I touch you?

Because I want to kiss you first.

Madeleine laughed.

You want to kiss me?

Yeah.

Okay.

He leaned toward her, his eyes closed and he placed his lips gently on hers. She began to laugh again.

Stop laughing, he said, pulling back.

I'm sorry, I can't help it. I've still got the giggles.

He pulled her close to him, saying, you shouldn't wear so much make-up.

I like wearing a lot of make-up.

But you're pretty and without make-up, I could see you better.

Maddy, very stoned, thought this was funny and began giggling again. It was dark out. Other cars with other teenagers sat parked around them. He began kissing her, more firmly, licking the corners of her mouth and sucking gently on her tongue. She felt herself relax. She had never kissed anyone before, not there on the mouth, not really kissed.

6

The first time Mark gave Maddy head they were in his bedroom and his parents were out to dinner at his aunt's house. His sisters were out God knows where. Maddy and he had been going out, fucking in his Chevy Nova, for a few months. It was a special occasion having the house, doing it in a bed. They were naked and the only light was from a streetlight outside and it lit up her large bones nicely. He could see the riverlike stretchmarks on her breasts and stomach, how the inside of her thighs sagged delicately. She lay on her back, her strong arms stretched above her head and he kissed her breasts and put his tongue in her navel and then, using both hands, spread her thighs apart, spread her cunt apart and he could feel her muscles tighten and was about to put his face in it when she sat up, looking confused and said, wait.

What, he said. She huffed and looked away and put fingers in her mouth. He said, don't you want me to and she said nothing. He put his face there and licked gently and she moaned and pulled away again. He said, what's wrong. She said, I'm embarrassed, really quietly, not like herself.

Whenever Maddy and he fucked she grunted lustily. She swore at him and sneered almost cruelly when she gave him head. She sucked his dick with a passion. She was a slut, a sex specialist, a high school whore. She wore the tightest jeans and the brightest make-up. She never smiled and no one scared her. Other kids made fun of him for fucking her, saying, you're going to get a disease, that girl's pussy is rank, she fucks everybody, she's a skanky ho. But he didn't care and now he knew he was waiting for that moment when her face would light up all scared and all her hardness melted away and her voice became so little and she had never had anybody eat her out or make her come.

He gave her head that night and he had her smeared all over his face and his nose burned from breathing out of it, his teeth were numb and his lips swollen and he made her come so hard that she cried. Big scary sobs, wordless words, whole sentences that made no sense. Her pussy swelled and shook and she grabbed his back and tore holes in his skin and screamed so loud he knew the neighbors heard her.

He had her. He had the girl no one else could have and no one wanted because she was such used trash but he had her in a way no one had ever had her. He broke her shell and what was inside was so pink and so vulnerable it scared him at first. Then he liked it. Then he loved it. Then he knew what it was he had. He had her.

When they fucked she still slit her eyes and made noises and sometimes she'd still curse but it was different. She lost her meanness. They'd go to drive-in movies and instead of grabbing his cock with her teeth gritted, she'd smile all shyly at him and sometimes she'd put his hand between her legs and give him this pleading look. All she ever wanted was head. She perfumed her cunt with peach-flavored lotion and powdered it with honey-tasting powder and shaved it and wore silky underwear with little bows on them. Pink panties and a black garter or a red G-string that went right up the crack of her ass like a strand of licorice. She spread her legs so wide and said Mark, give it to me, that's it, don't stop, oh God don't stop. He watched her change so quickly and she changed just for him because she still walked around that school with her eyes all hard and her make-up too bright and the thick seam of her jeans rudely splaying her cunt lips apart, her hips jutted forward. But she'd take one look at his skinny ass in the hallway and all that hardness melted away like butter. She stumbled over her words and blushed and fidgeted and would whisper and giggle in Mark's ear like a virgin. People said what are you doing with that disgusting ho bag but he never listened to them because he knew her soft side and it was so soft it seemed it could disappear.

He'd make her beg for it say please Mark, say pretty please and she'd say it with her voice quivering, her cheeks all hot and red. He'd say, what are you going to do for me and she'd say anything, anything. He said let me fuck you in the ass and she'd say okay, okay. And she'd roll onto her stomach and lift her hips into the air, her pink, crinkly holes right out in the open and say, get the KY, her head pressed into the pillow, her voice all muffled.

That's when she started to show him her tricks. She put her fingers inside herself for him and she said, I can do more. If I show you will you eat me? She said, I used to do it alone at home. She said, now I'll do it for you, don't you want to see it? She put her fingers in there and then her hand, concentrating, eyes wide and her mouth stretched open like her cunt. He said let me do it, Maddy, and she'd say do it and he put his fingers in her and then his hand. He put all sorts of things inside of her. Her breathing would become deep and regular, so rhythmic and steady, like a swimmer or something and her eyes became focused inward, wide open, glazed, never blinking. He tied her legs apart, her knees bent up and he put a fist or a shoe in her and she'd exhale so so slowly and close her eyes.

And she'd say now will you give it to me, now will you eat

me Mark, yeah, yeah, now give it to me, looking up at me, her eyes begging, her mouth shaking, a Coke bottle in her cunt and a vibrator in her ass. So then he gave it to her—He'd give her head and she'd grab his hair, move him around until he sucked just that right spot and she'd scream unearthly things, their bodies turned around again and again until he lay underneath her cunt, her soft thighs grabbing his cheeks.

But how long can you eat a girl out? How long can you taste her thick and wet metal skin that's so soft it's almost not there? She still cried occasionally. She still came hard. But not always. Sometimes there'd be the littlest shake and peep out of her and she'd get off his face or pull him up and say that's it, Mark, that's it. How many things can you stick inside of a girl? How long can you look at her, her pussy slick and misshapen, stretching this way and that around every godforsaken object in the house? How long does it takes before all of those special moments, those wet eyes, those weak lips, the line of sweat between the breasts, all those things stop coming? How long before she yawns and watches TV later than you, before she'd rather talk on the phone? How long before it all ends and Madeleine, although she tries and tries, stops being what she used to be, starts being just another person, just another wife with a job, eating potato chips on the couch?

7

Madeleine and Mark lay in the backseat of his Nova after having fucked. The windows were steamed. They were naked, except

Maddy had kept on her black garter belt and fishnet stockings. She absentmindedly tucked her fleshy thighs into the tops of her stockings.

Why are you so nice to me? Maddy asked.

Because I like you.

I'm the kind of girl your mother tells you to stay away from, she said, sitting up and putting on a light blue tank top.

Who listens to their mothers, said Mark, grabbing her playfully, while he tried to pull down her top. She pushed his hand away.

I know people at school make fun of you.

Jesus, Maddy. You think I care?

Well, I'd just hate to see you regret acting this way with me.

I'm not acting, Maddy. I like you a lot. You're special.

You don't even know how special I am, she said, grinning.

Well, I think I know but I'm sure there are things I don't know. And I want to know everything about you. Anyway, I know people say shit to you about hanging out with me.

I don't listen to anybody.

You do. All your freak loser friends.

Fuck you, I do not.

Then why don't you kiss me in the hallway at school?

I don't know, she said, turning her head to face out the foggy window.

You don't let me touch you in public.

I will if you want.

I do. I want that.

Mark's face was eager and he tried turning her head away from the window.

Stop staring out the window. You can't see out it. You're just avoiding me.

Maddy turned to face him.

You just like fucking me.

I like fucking you and I like you. You're not fucking anyone else anymore, either.

How do you know, she said icily, her teeth closed against each other.

I would know if you were fucking someone else. We talk or see each other constantly.

Well maybe we should change that.

I don't want to change that. I like always knowing what you're doing.

Maybe it's making you cocky.

Maddy, I'm not trying to be cocky.

You don't own me.

I know I don't own you. But you are my girlfriend.

I don't know if I feel comfortable with that, she said, sliding into the front seat, let's go. Take me home.

Well, it's the truth, Maddy, you are my girlfriend, Mark said. He jumped into the driver's seat and started the car, saying, when people talk all the time and fuck all the time and like each other a lot, they're boyfriend and girlfriend.

You're so sure of yourself, she said sarcastically and she turned the radio on and turned the volume up loud.

I'm not so sure of myself, he said, almost screaming so he could be heard over the music, I just know we're a couple. That's all.

8

Mark left town to go to a cousin's wedding. Madeleine called up Carrie and asked her if she wanted to go ice skating. She said, let's go to Eric's party instead. Maddy said, I'll go to his party. But let's skate first just for the fuck of it. She said, I'll pick you up . . . wait, don't you got some boyfriend? Maddy said, yeah, so what, let's go out?

Carrie picked her up in her father's car. They sat in the parking lot and drank from a bright green bottle of peppermint schnapps which Carrie had stolen from her dad and smoked a pin joint. Carrie and Maddy didn't really go to the rink anymore. Carrie went to parties and Maddy was always with Mark. Carrie's hair was dyed brassy orange and pressed super straight with an iron. She said, you're serious with this boyfriend, huh? Maddy said yeah, kind of. She said, it's some nerd, right, and Maddy said, yeah. She started laughing. She said, how can you fuck some nerd and Maddy told her to shut up.

The schnapps hit Maddy's head like green fire. She was drunk, huge, bigger than the world. She was sticking her tits out, she was high, feeling good. They skated around, the lights were real bright. Oz was still working there. The Zamboni pulled out on the ice and Carrie and Maddy started heading to the bathroom to smoke another pinner. Then Oz walked up with some new rink guard and said, hey you guys want to smoke a joint with us? They said, sure.

They all went into the rink guard station. A stack of Hustlers sat on the table. The new rink guard, Jimmy, was younger than Oz, closer to Maddy and Carrie's age. He went to the high school. He had a peach fuzz face and a squeaky nervous laugh. He kept sticking a finger in his ear and then sniffing his finger. He had a southern accent. He kept saying, in Kentucky, there's the best weed and it's so much cheaper and in Kentucky this or that. He spit on the floor.

They went back out to the rink, stoned. Maddy's mouth was swollen dry and everything moved slowly. Carrie said, that new guy's cute, right? Yeah, I guess, Maddy said, but he talks too much about Kentucky. Carrie said, should we ask them to go out after the rink closes? Maddy said, sure, why not.

The boys said, yeah, we'll go. They said, yeah we know Eric, we were gonna go anyway.

Eric's father didn't live with him and his mother was a cocktail waitress who wasn't coming home until four in the morning. Maddy'd blown him and most of his friends and she hadn't really seen them in a long time except quickly in the hallways at school. She still looked at all the guys and they still looked at her, but she just stopped talking to them. She stopped walking up to them. They'd just glance at each other in the hallway. Occasionally somebody'd yell something like, suck my dick, Maddy. Or, where've you been, Mad girl, with that dickless fag again? She never cared much what they said, but she still cared about the way they looked at her. She still cared about that.

Well, look who's here, hey guys, check it out, Madeleine's here, Eric said, opening the door for them. Carrie said, Hi Eric, aren't you gonna say anything to me? No, he said, I see your face all the time.

The music was loud. There was a keg in the kitchen. The lights were low and a blue light hung in an empty back room. There were a few other girls there from the high school and about fifteen guys. Oz and Jimmy came in. Carrie pulled Maddy close and whispered, I think I'm going to go for that guy Jimmy, what do you think? Maddy said sure, go for it.

There was still some schnapps left. Maddy drank it real fast, chased it with beer. Her head spun and reeled and she gritted her teeth to balance herself. Carrie and Maddy sat on the couch next to each other. Carrie lit another joint and Oz and Jimmy came over and they smoked. Carrie said, so Jimmy, you got a girlfriend? He said, no. She said, you're real cute. He started glancing around nervously. He was standing in front of the couch and he sat down on the armrest, next to her, his legs spread wide, his hands resting on his knees.

He said, in Kentucky, I had a girlfriend. Carrie said, yeah, what was her name? He said, Ashley. She said, that's a pretty name—do you miss her? He said, yeah, but not so much as I did. Do you write her? Yeah, he said, I used to write her a lot.

Do you call her? Yeah, not too much. What'd she look like? Carrie asked. I got a picture of her he said, standing up.

Jimmy reached into his back pocket, standing up in front of Carrie, his jeans super tight against his crotch. He pulled out his wallet and took out a photo and sat down again on the armrest. He gave the photo to Carrie. She said, oh, she's pretty and passed the photo to Maddy. Isn't she pretty, Maddy?

It was a yearbook photo, with a sky blue background. The girl had dyed blond hair that was long and curly. She wore a tight yellow sweater—her bra all stiff and pointy underneath it. Her teeth were crooked. Maddy turned the photo over and on the back it said, Jimmy, I will love you forever, love, Ashley. Her handwriting was big and swirly, barely fitting on the back of the photo.

Jimmy snatched the photo back, stood up again and put it back in his wallet. Carrie, said again, she's real pretty, Jimmy. You must miss her. She had a smirk on her face. Maddy felt her face get hot. Carrie said, did she treat you nicely, Jimmy? Did she treat you right? Yeah, he said, looking at her stiffly. You wanna marry her, don't you? He said, yeah. Did she touch you here, Jimmy, Carrie said, and slick as butter her hand was on the bulge tightly encased in his jeans, so quickly you barely saw her hand move but she clasped on like it was always there—her palm underneath his balls, her fingers stretching over his cock.

She wasn't a ho like you, he said, his voice thick. Maddy watched his cock grow harder under his jeans, under her friend's thin hand and she felt herself get wet. Did she fuck you, Jimmy?

Carrie squeezed hard. I didn't fuck her, he said, not moving, I made love to her. Ah, so she did treat you nice, Carrie said, taking her hand off his cock and sitting back on the couch. I thought I had me a nice virgin boy.

He stuck his jaw out. You slut, he said, dragging the word out long with his Kentucky drawl. But he didn't leave.

You ever fuck anyone else besides Ashley? Carrie asked, her eyes perking upward on her forehead. Shut up, you fucking whore, Jimmy said, but still he didn't move away from her and his cock was still hard in his pants. She ever suck your dick, huh Jimmy, she ever put your dick in her pretty little mouth? Jimmy said nothing. She said, let me take you in the back room. Carrie stood up and reached for his hand but he pulled away from her, jerked away from her. She was all little bones and sharp angles, hands on her hips. She said, I know you're gonna follow me, and she started walking to that back room with the blue light and no one in it. He got up and followed her and shut the door behind them.

The seat of Maddy's pants were wet, her crotch burned against her jeans. She got up and walked to the keg to pour herself a beer and fell down. Eric and some friends of his helped her up. Maddy said, I'm just trying to get to the keg. Eric said, you sit on the couch and I'll bring you a beer. She sat back down. Eric brought her a beer and Oz came and sat down and there were others there, too. Maddy said, thanks, Eric, nice party—and drank her beer.

You're still a whore even though you never come here anymore, Eric said.

Fuck you very much, she said.

Where's your pussy boyfriend?

He's at his cousin's wedding.

Why didn't he take you?

I don't know.

Maybe you're too big of a whore to take to a wedding. You probably can't walk into a church without it burning down.

She said nothing.

You are one drunk bitch.

Fuck you very much.

Why'd you come here tonight? Felt like sucking some dick?

I came here cause Carrie wanted to come here.

Carrie's sucking some dick right now. Ain't that right?

Everyone started yelping and laughing.

Eric said, let's check out Carrie's dick sucking. You know, he said, leaning over to her, she never sucked cock as good as you did. Suck my dick Maddy, he said, breathing warmly on her. Right here. His voice was soft and his eyes looked vulnerable. He pulled his dick out of his jeans and everyone started to howl.

She said, get that away from me.

He said, you never came into my house before without sucking my dick.

She said, well, this will be a first.

Bitch! After you drink my beer. Shit, after I go and get you a beer and bring it to you like you're some fucking princess.

I am a princess.

You're a pig, he said, putting his dick back in his pants and he grabbed her face, squeezing her cheeks so hard it hurt and her lips stuck out. She tried pulling back but he held on tight. He said, you're a ho and a big-assed pig.

They were all around her. She saw some of the other girls from the high school, watching on, being jealous. They were sluts and they weren't getting the attention they were used to. She was getting it all. She knew it was just because she hadn't been around in a long time. So she seemed special.

Some guy said, hey let's go see how Carrie's doing, and he walked over and opened the door to the back room. The blue light was still on. Everyone turned toward the room. Maddy got up and stumbled and almost fell but steadied herself on some guy. She pushed past some guys to see because the door to the back room was surrounded now.

She saw Carrie laying spread eagle on the floor and Jimmy straddling her head, his bare ass tightened up and facing everybody. Carrie had all her clothes on. She had his cock in her mouth. Everyone hooted. Jimmy stood up, shoving his pants over his hard dick. Carrie propped herself up on her elbows and started to laugh, her chin wet and shiny. Eric walked in and then another and another and Oz was in there too and Maddy walked away and watched Jimmy go out the front door, his face bright red and lips puffy. Maddy walked over to the couch and lay down for a while and tried to rest her eyes but the noise of them wouldn't let her and then she went in the bathroom and threw up.

Eric was standing outside of the bathroom when she got out.

You puke? he asked. She didn't say anything—she just tried to get by him. You should go help your friend out. The ho can't take them all by herself. Yes she can, Maddy said. Carrie's taken a party twice this size and there are other girls here, too. He said, you've taken parties bigger than this. Maddy said, I don't anymore. He said, what's wrong with you? You don't like dick anymore? She said, shut up Eric. He smiled, a chipped tooth and hard lips and his eyes like mud. He said you did it better. You're made for hoing. Your big roomy mouth and ass. But you've lost some weight. I bet it's because you don't get enough.

Let me go by, I'm going home.

How're you getting home? Carrie's not driving you anywhere.

I can walk. It's not far.

Let me drive you home.

You're drunk as shit.

I'll walk you home.

I'm not sucking your dick.

Fine let me just walk you home.

He moved around, from one foot to another.

I don't want you to walk me home, Eric.

What if I said I wanted you to be my girlfriend?

I'd say you were lying.

Really, Maddy.

I've got a boyfriend.

That fag you hang out with?

I'm on my way home, get out of my way.

She pushed him aside and he started yelling after her. Whore, cocksucker, fuck socket, hobag. VD-having, stinking, rotting cunt. Don't come back to my house ever again.

She walked home and it took a while. She threw up again in some bushes on the way. She wanted Mark to come back and to smell him and feel him and she wanted to tell him that they still beg for it from her, they still want her and what do you think about that Mark? I'm yours and I'm the slut of all sluts. She wanted to say, Markie you haven't taken it away from me I still have it. I still have what it takes. She thought, I could show you my insides, I could turn myself inside out for you, me, me, who everybody wants, me, who can swallow the whole world. But when he came back she didn't say anything. They kissed, they held each other, they made love. Maddy said let's move in together and he said okay. He said let's get married when we graduate.

9

They told her parents first, standing side by side and then they drove over to his parents' house, side by side, and told them. Afterwards Maddy straddled him in the car, pushing the full weight of herself against him. He felt crushed, suffocated, over-whelmed. She fucked him like that, sitting on top of him. She said, do you love me. Yes, he said. Oh, I love you she said, oh, contracting her muscles around his cock, moving forward and back again, saying does this feel good? Yeah, Maddy. Yeah. He came inside of her and then he pushed her off, quickly, aggressively, and laying her against the seat, he pulled her hips up to his face and ate her until she begged him to stop. His own come dripping down his chin, he dropped her off at her house and went home and went to bed.

The next day they went to City Hall. Maddy wore a short white dress and had her hair combed down demurely instead of frizzed out. She wore hardly any make-up. His parents talked awkwardly with hers. Mark and Maddy were married. It didn't take long. Everybody signed a piece of paper. They planned on saving money and going on a honeymoon when they could afford to go somewhere special. That night, they rented a room at the Marriot Hotel, the nicest hotel in South Bend. They ordered a bottle of champagne and then another and then another. They fucked and fucked again and by the third bottle of champagne and the third time he entered her, they were laughing. They started laughing so hard and Mark's cock went limp and fell out of her.

Oh, baby, look you're bored of me already. We've been married less than a day and already you're bored of me, Maddy said and she pushed him on his back and started giving him head, hoping to revive his erection.

No, no. I'm not bored of you baby. I'm just drunk.

Maddy pulled his cock out of her mouth for a moment, saying, you've fucked me when you were drunk before.

I just fucked you twice.

He lay back, feeling her on him, her mouth working away, but he was not aroused. Come up here and kiss me, he said and she flopped next to him. He leaned over and licked her neck, saying, how could you ever bore me?

I don't know.

You could never bore me. I just swore my life to you. I fucking worship you.

The next morning they took a long bath together and ordered breakfast delivered to the room. They watched a movie, hungover and tired, and checked out of the hotel an hour late. Maddy had found an apartment and Mark said okay and they were planning on moving in that day.

10

Their apartment was perfectly fine and in a decent neighborhood. It was the top floor of an old house. They had a separate entrance and could park the car in the driveway. There was a tree in the front yard and some grass. Maddy hadn't looked for long—maybe she could have found something a little bigger further away from the central part of the town. But they couldn't wait. They were eighteen and impatient. Maddy got really excited about it, cooking and cleaning and buying lace curtains for the bedroom. They smoked pot in the living room, had sex in the kitchen.

The air didn't move around well in the apartment. This bothered Mark. He took it as a bad omen, but he didn't say anything
to her. There was no cross circulation.

He had never spent so much time with someone in such a
small place. He had had his own room at home. Every night she
lay next to him. Every morning he woke up next to her.

The place didn't contain Maddy that well. Before, Maddy
and Mark spent a lot of time in his car, or at his parents' house
if no one was home. Or they went out to eat, sitting in some
booth. Everything and every place had been momentary, transi-
tory. But once they had their own place, time stopped and he
learned new things about her.

She walked around in the apartment, back and forth, back
and forth. Into the kitchen, out to the living room, into the
bedroom back to the kitchen picking up this, putting away that
and always cooking. Her face was in the fridge or in a drawer or
in a cabinet. Her hands wrapped around a bowl of cookie dough
or a vacuum cleaner or a basket of laundry.

When they sat around together, smoking and drinking on the
dark green couch (a gift from her parents), watching a movie, he
could feel her next to him. She'd get up during commercials and
go into the kitchen—do whatever—go into the bedroom, fluff
a pillow. If they were watching a video and there were no commercials—she'd get up anyway. He'd say, Maddy, you want me
to press pause? She didn't give a shit. She'd say, no that's alright,
and go into the bathroom and put green stuff on her face. I'm
just putting on a facial, she'd say. I'll be right out. And he'd hear

her tinkering around in there. He'd hear the cabinet shut and open and shut and open and the water run. He wouldn't be able to pay attention to the movie. He'd miss what happened.

Then she got pregnant. She went off the pill without telling him.

When she told him, she was excited and red in the face and ashamed. Sweetie, she said, I'm pregnant. No way. Not until we have money. I'm nineteen, he said. We're too young. He took a day off of work to drive her to the clinic. She sat silently next to him. Her face was puffy from crying.

I don't want to get an abortion.

I know, honey.

I'm scared.

Maddy bit the palm of her hand and looked at Mark hunched over the wheel.

I'll be with you, he said.

They won't let you past the waiting room.

I'll be there when you get out.

I know. But I'm still scared, she said, the pitch of her voice altered. Her palms were salty and slick And she sucked on one of them.

Don't be scared, Maddy. It's a quick operation. It's much less dangerous than childbirth. You don't even have to go under.

I know. It's not that shit that bothers me.

Mark shifted in aggitation, saying, well, what's bothering you?

I'm just not excited about this okay.

We can't have a baby.

I know. You're right. I was wrong. I don't want to have a baby. I just don't want to have an abortion, she said and she started to cry. Mark pulled over.

Oh, honey don't cry. In a few hours this will all be over, he said. He tried to lean toward her—to kiss her.

Get away from me.

Don't be mad at me, Maddy.

I am.

This is not my fault.

So it's mine?

Go back on the pill.

I'm going to, she said. Mark started driving again. They pulled into a parking lot.

We're here.

Oh shit. Oh shit. I'm scared.

It's okay. Come on. Let's go.

Maddy sat in the interior waiting room, separated from her husband who had to wait in the outside waiting room. She bounced her leg around nervously. Her stomach felt sour. She looked at a magazine. A thick, cruel looking girl sat across from her.

Is this your first one? the girl asked, cracking her gum loudly.

Excuse me?

You can always tell the ones that haven't had one. You look scared. Don't worry. It ain't nothing. I've had eight.

Nurse. Nurse, excuse me? Can I move back to the outside waiting room, Maddy said, standing up, chasing down a nurse coming toward her. The nurse was not much older than Maddy, wore no make-up and had dark hair pulled back tightly in a ponytail. She looked at Maddy with a professionally toned friendliness and pity.

No, I'm sorry. You're next.

I need to talk to my husband.

You can go into room five now. The doctor will be right with you.

I'm scared, Maddy said and started to cry.

It's okay. It will be over before you know it, the doctor replied. Maddy had requested a female doctor. The woman was from Eastern Europe and spoke with a harsh accent and had a perpetual scowl across her lined face.

Oh shit.

Don't cry, the doctor ordered.

It hurts.

It's almost over.

Oh, it hurts. Oh jesus!

Sshh. Quiet! Tell her to be quiet, the doctor said, glaring at the nurse.

You heard the doctor. Quiet down. Sshhh. That's it. Ssshh. There you go. You're all done.

I want to see it.

Stop that. Don't move. Stay still.

How big is it?

Sit back. Sshhh. Come on.

Stop her crying.

I want to see it.

Sssshhhh.

Maddy was stoned on pain relievers and asked for more juice in the post-op waiting room. The same dark-haired nurse brought her a tiny paper cup filled with cranberry juice.

Here you go.

Thanks.

The nurse smoothed her ponytail and asked, do you still want to know how big it was?

Yeah.

It was this big, she said, holding her thumb and forefinger apart in front of Maddy's face, about an inch and a half. You were seven weeks pregnant.

Okay. Thanks.

Mark drove her home and she kept her head in his lap the whole way.

What movie did you rent?

The Getaway. How're you feeling?

Okay.

Do you want me to order a pizza?

Okay.

Are you cold?

No. Hey Mark?

What sweetie?

It was this big.

What?

It was this big. One and a half inches.

Don't think about it.

The day after the abortion she broke all the plates in the kitchen and emptied the food in the fridge on the floor. Then she took three Codeine pills and went to bed. He heard her wake in the night and vomit.

Mark decided to keep her birth control pills after in a drawer in her desk. He was the one to go to the drug store and buy them. Every morning he made her take one. He woke her and watched her swallow it. He made her stick her tongue out at him, he'd look down the back of her throat. Sometimes he ran his finger around the inside of her mouth. We're not going through that again, ever, he'd say. She didn't protest.

After a month of that, she said, stop checking on me, Mark. I don't want to get pregnant. Really, don't worry about me, she said. He told her when we're older and more settled that they'd have a family. He'd say Maddy, if you had a kid you wouldn't be able to party anymore. Your whole life would be taking care of the kid. You're too young. And she'd cry and say I know Mark, I know, you're right, it just breaks my heart.

. . .

11

At first, she thought their apartment was great. Sure, it wasn't very big but it was theirs and they had a couch and a TV and their own bed and her mom bought them plates and flatware and glasses. She got a job waitressing and he worked in a computer store at the mall and had all his computers.

She bought *The Joy of Cooking* and *Cooking for Two* and *Cooking on a Budget*. She went grocery shopping at Krogers and filled her spice rack with cheerful bottles of dried herbs. Oregano, basil, thyme, sage, cinnamon, nutmeg. She bought breakfast cereals and English muffins and Oscar Meyer luncheon meats and packed his lunch in brown bags. At night, if she wasn't working she made dinner and she ate with him. They had a VCR. She thought they had everything.

She painted the bedroom walls an apricot and the bathroom baby blue. The living room walls were white and the kitchen she wallpapered with a flowered print that reminded her of the kitchen at home. They had a La-Z-Boy chair that he sat in when he came home and put his feet up and smoked pot and watched TV. On Saturdays she vacuumed and Ajaxed the bathroom and did the laundry. She had a white plastic laundry basket and she'd fold everything up, even his underwear. Neat, little stacks, all lined up and clean. She washed the whites separate from the colors and used enough bleach to get it white white, but not too much so nothing ever yellowed and the material wouldn't get stiff. She ironed. She did everything she could do.

He liked meatloaf and pork chops and mashed potatoes with nutmeg in them. He liked salted butter. He liked turkey sandwiches and roast beef on rye. She wiped the top of the fridge off so dust never collected there. She wiped the dust off the TV screen and his computer screens and keyboards.

He bought her presents at first. He bought her red roses and lingerie and high heeled shoes. He took her out to dinner and afterward he drove her to Howard Park and they made out in the car, like they did way back when.

She loved him. She loved everything about him. She loved his plain brown hair that hung straight and that he kept short even though she asked him to grow it long. She loved his pale face and thin mouth and his liquid, colorless eyes. She loved his thin arms that curved inward between his elbows and knobby shoulders. She loved the tan hairs that grew on his body and his brown, shapeless nipples and his dark, deep bellybutton. His almost wide hips and round ass. His armpits, barely hairy that smelled of him.

She loved his smell like it was the most important, safe thing that she ever smelled. Like the smell of him could keep her from what was bad in her and what was bad in the world. She smelled him next to her at night with her mouth open and she breathed him in through the skin on her body, through every pore in her face and she put her face against his back at night and listened to his lungs open and close.

She loved the way he put the key in the door when he came home. The way he put his bag down and kicked off his shoes right there in the kitchen. The way he moved his stuff around on the desk, all that stuff around his computer, all the things he kept so neat, how he seemed to need to touch it all, make sure it was all there. She loved the way he ate and the way he sat and the sound of his breath while he slept.

Her love for him grew each damn day. Her love for him grew so strong there wasn't any room for anything else. Her love grew strong and she tired, tired of how it took everything from her—her soft hands, her clear brow, the curve of her hips, the smile on her face.

The more she thought of him the more it hurt her. The more she loved him the more she had to steal from him. Steal looks at him. Steal her hands over his back while he slept. Steal time away from him, steal time with him.

Absence makes the heart grow fonder. Out of sight out of mind. If he thought she didn't need him then maybe he'd want to kiss her as badly as he wanted to kiss her that first time in the car. He was the only man she ever kissed. If he didn't know how miserable she was without him maybe he'd think she was strong and sure like she once had been. If she acted tough there was a chance she was tough. If she didn't show her pain then maybe it wasn't there.

She acted like she didn't love him anymore. It seemed like it was all gone. But it was there, she just tried to keep it contained, tried to show him she was still the same Maddy.

The air in the apartment became stiff, no matter how high the fan was on. No matter what she cooked the kitchen smelled stale. Dinner on the stove smelled like heaven while her face was in the pan, but once that was over, once she put the food down to eat in front of the TV, the stale smell took over again. She couldn't eat, no matter what she cooked. Vegetables were like rubber in her mouth, bright and plastic. Chicken tasted like slime, no matter how she prepared it. She'd gag trying to force it down. Mark ate and ate. He gained weight. She lost weight. She began vacuuming every day, thinking maybe it was the carpet that smelled stale. She used carpet fresheners; floral scents, spring scents, pine scents. Sprinkling the sharp, scented white powder on the dreary wall to wall carpet, chasing it around with the vacuum cleaner. She dusted and put her nose to the furniture after wiping it down with lemon Pledge.

The longer she lived with him the less recognizable he became. His face, his body, what would come out of his mouth. What was going on in his head. The expressions on his face. He grew out of focus, strange and foreign.

Their apartment never had been cleaner. There wasn't a speck of dust anywhere, a mislaid sock anywhere. The fridge smelled like a fresh box of baking soda and the chrome in the bathroom gleamed. She tried every recipe in every cookbook. Sometimes she went through them alphabetically. Pork Chops Almondine, Pork Chops Barbecue, Pork Chops Catherine. The freezer was full of homemade frozen dinners in Tupperware and various other food stuffs wrapped in aluminum foil. She cooked and cooked and cleaned and cleaned until her fingers were pink and raw from water and soap and rubbing up against things. But she stopped being hungry altogether.

It wasn't like the time when she first started dieting when she was a kid and was forced to do it. Then it was hard and she missed eating so much. This time, it was just the opposite. Hunger left her first.

She didn't want to eat and not eating gave her pleasure and made her feel stronger. The less she ate the less she wanted to eat. She felt blessed. She felt special.

Air tasted different and smells became stronger and everything became more textured. Sometimes the smell of a hamburger that she was cooking for Mark was so strong and sweet that she almost cried, so overcome by its power. A fresh washed blanket against her face felt like a cloud from heaven and smelled as sweet as talc. She felt thankful to be alive.

Her legs grew longer, or so it seemed. Her stomach became flat and the lines on her skin, the wrinkles she'd always had from losing weight when she was younger, became stronger and more defined. Dark, jagged lines running across her body, the flesh hanging loosely around them. She traced them over and over again. They comforted her.

For the most part she stopped sleeping more than a few hours a night. She'd lie next to him, like she always had, but now she tried to recognize him, tried to remember who he was to her.

And as she stared at his back in the dark, bent toward her

in their bed, memories did come. But she didn't trust them. The images were vague and as she tried to bring them into focus in her mind, she would get startled and think—is that his face I'm imagining leaning to kiss me and then she would wonder, but is that his nose? Are those his lips? And indeed they weren't because she would slip around the bed and stare at his face, breathing deeply and no, his nose was different. His lips, stretched out in sleep, were rubbery and non-distinct. So she had imagined, remembered, the wrong nose and the wrong cheekbones. The face she crouched in front of in their bedroom was longer and thinner, the bones high and narrow. In her mind he had a rounder face, a pink hue, a broadness to his cheeks.

So she would press her face against him and smell him like she had, like she remembered doing and often what came back to her was too strong to bear and she would pull back, her nostrils burning.

Her memories lied to her. She became convinced she had conjured visions for her own needs of comfort. She didn't know a bone in his body and her own were shifting slowly, steadily.

She stared at the sink and she stared at the dishtowels and she watched the television and occasionally they looked at each other and occasionally there would be a sign of comfort, a signal of recognition and caring, but more often they ignored each other.

And that smell. The staleness. It became so strong she could barely stay in the house. If she wasn't busy cooking or cleaning she sat in front of an open window and stuck her face out to breathe the fresh air. She was terrified and the only thing that subdued her fear while she was in that apartment was her ability to not eat.

She began working extra waitressing shifts to get out of the house. She worked brunches and doubles during the week when she could. Adding checks and taking orders and filling ketchups with a newfound organization and efficiency. Her boss loved her. She always filled all the salt and pepper shakers and wiped down all the menus. The other waitresses loved her. They could always count on her to cover a shift, even if they called at the last minute because they were hungover and didn't want to work. She'd rush off to work, her uniform spotless and ironed. She washed it lovingly in the sink every night, carefully rubbing out stains and hung it on her bedroom door, ready to be pressed and worn first thing in the morning.

She accumulated tons of cash. She wrapped a rubber band around each stack of five hundred dollars and put them in long, white envelopes that she sealed and hid in her underwear drawer—which she then locked. She saved thousands of dollars in a matter of months.

Her plans for the money changed. She thought of moving to California or New York. She thought of buying a gun or a car or a house. She knew whatever she spent it on, it would just be on her, not Mark. And she wasn't saving for a baby. Sometimes he'd ask, what are you doing working all the time? He'd ask, what are you doing with all that money? Once he even said sweetly, let's go on a vacation, on our honeymoon baby, we both have the money to do it. She ignored him.

And then the fights began.

12

Mark came home from work and put his bag down and kicked off his shoes. He walked into the living room and Maddy was sitting on the couch with her arms folded over her chest. He knew she was angry. She almost always was.

I'm not doing those dishes, she said.

Fine, I'll do them, he said, his voice remaining calm, despite the anxiety mounting in his head.

She stood up and said, why didn't you do them a week ago? Why'd you have to let them sit there for a week and stink up our kitchen and let the food get hard on them so that now when you do do them the shit will be impossible to get off? Huh? You were waiting for me to do them, right?

You are on the rag, he said and walked into the bedroom and threw himself down on the bed. He couldn't take it. Her constant bitching. Maddy followed him and stood at the end of the bed, looking down at him.

Fuck you. You're an unappreciative pig and I'm sick of wiping up after you. Grow the fuck up.

Get out of my face.

You should apologize to me and ask me how you can help me. You should ask me what you can do around here.

You're being a bitch, Maddy, do you know that?

I'm pissed.

Calm down.

You fucking calm down. You don't do shit in this house. I do everything.

He said, I've asked you before what can I do around here and you always say, oh nothing sweetie. And now for whatever reason you want to yell at me. So fucking yell at me.

He got up and tried to walk out of the room but she stood in the doorway, blocking him. The skin on her face drooped strangely. He said, I'm going out until you calm down.

She said, you're not leaving here until you do those goddamn dishes.

Get out of my way, he said and pushed her out of the way. She followed him into the kitchen and watched him put his shoes back on. Fuck you and your dishes, he said.

You're not going anywhere, Mark, she seethed, standing in front of the door.

Get out of my way, Maddy, I'm serious.

What are you going to do, hit me?

Is that what you want? That's probably what you want, you sick bitch. I'll do it, Maddy. I'm not scared of you.

You touch me and I'll beat the living shit out of you.

Mark grabbed her arms, saying, you're not that tough

anymore, Maddy. Look at you. You've lost so much weight you can't even lift a bag of groceries.

She shook free of him. It's not that I can't lift a bag of groceries, Mark, it's that I won't lift a bag of groceries. I'm sick of doing everything here.

Get out of my way, I'm leaving, he said and pushed her out of his way again. She stumbled and caught herself on the kitchen counter.

Where are you going?

None of your fucking business, he said as he walked out the door and down the stairs.

Mark, damn you. Mark, wait, come back. I'm sorry. Come back. I'm *sorry*, Mark. I'll cook dinner.

13

If she didn't yell at him about the dishes then she yelled at him about the floors. If she didn't yell at him about that, she yelled at him for not paying attention to her, for never buying her flowers or chocolates or taking her out to dinner. He'd say, Maddy, you'd throw the chocolates out, you'd sniff them for a day and then throw them out. It's the thought that counts, she'd say. If I took you out to dinner you'd order a salad and then not eat it. You'd move it around on your plate. Then take me out and let's get drunk, she'd say. He'd say, you'd get drunk after two beers because you're so goddamn skinny and then you'd start yelling and crying at me. She'd say, what's your excuse for not buying me flowers? He'd say, last time I bought you flowers, you threw them at me. I can't remember why. But you were angry at me. Fuck you, Mark, she'd cry. You just don't love me anymore. That's not true, Maddy, he'd say. I love you like crazy, you're being impossible.

Or if he tried cleaning—and their place was too clean, she was always cleaning—but if he tried to help out then she'd be behind him in a second, grabbing the sponge from his hand, saying, you're not doing it right, you stupid fuck. So he'd try and do things when she was at work, which wasn't difficult because she was always at work. It didn't mattter. When she came home she'd clean the entire apartment, banging every-thing around, swearing under her breath and Mark would just leave the apartment. What was he supposed to do? He'd buy her a pair of lacy panties. And she'd thank him. But that was it. Nothing else. No wild fucking. No panting and grabbing. Not even a kiss. Thanks, Mark, and a brief, forced smile. Did she wear them ever? He would never find out. She changed in the bathroom or in the dark and walked around with a thick terrycloth robe pulled defensively over her body. I'm so tired from work, she'd say and pull the blankets over her. It felt use-less, every effort made. Is this because of the abortion, he'd ask, again. No, Mark, things were weird before that. Don't you think so? And he'd have to agree. She was right. But what should we do, how do we get over this, how do we get back to being crazy about each other? I don't know, she'd mumble, annoyed. Just don't worry about it so much. Things will get better. Maybe it's the stress of moving in together, she'd offer. We've been living together for almost a year, he'd say. Oh, Mark, drop it, I'm tired.

She pushed him away and then screamed at him for not being close. And then he just had to get away. So he went over to Nathan's house more and more. Sometimes he'd go there straight after work.

Nathan lived in a seedy neighborhood a few blocks from downtown. His apartment was on the ground floor, and there were big windows facing the street so Mark could drive by and see if the lights were on, see if Nathan was home. Which he almost always was. He sold pot out of his apartment and he did this mostly at night. He was in his thirties, had long, stringy hair and a goatee and there was something very greasy about him. He didn't wash often. He had no girlfriend or wife. He constantly made fun of Mark for being married. Nathan frequented whores and watched pornography nonstop. He had a library of movies and stacks and stacks of magazines. Stoned, drinking cheap beer out of a can, they'd sit around with some of his other friends and watch pornos. He had gang bangs. He had girls getting fucking by Great Danes. He had it all. All the new glossy ones and all the twisted underground and amateur ones.

Mark drove over and saw Nathan's lights on. He saw Larry's car parked out front. He went in, carrying a six pack, and sat down with the two of them. They passed around a bong. Mark bought a bag of weed from him. They smoked some more.

Your little woman drive you out of the house again? Nathan asked.

It's like she's on the rag all month long.

I'm telling you, you should get the fuck out of there. Fuck living with women. Just have them over to suck your dick once in a while, he said, coughing out a big bong hit. He said, whores are where it's at. There's a reason why it's the oldest profession.

I married a whore. I don't have to pay for one. But she's changed. She's not as fun as she used to be.

Larry said, that's cause once you marry her, she can't be your whore anymore. Now she's your wife. That shit's different.

Mark said, she's still a whore. She'll always be one. That's why I love her.

Larry said, man, I can't understand how you can call your wife a whore. That's fucked up. No wonder you have problems.

You guys don't get it, Mark said. They all looked quietly at the TV. A woman was getting fucked by three guys. One in her mouth, one in her ass, and one in her pussy.

Your wife do that shit? Nathan laughed, pointing to the TV.

My wife does anything.

Larry said, see you can't talk about your wife that way. He shook his head.

What rule book is that from? Mark asked sarcastically.

No really, it's common knowledge, Larry said. You can't think of your wife that way. You got to have respect.

We're special, Mark said, cracking open another beer, settling in for a long evening at Nathan's. We're not a boring, old fart couple. Ours is special. We're just having some problems.

But he went over to Nathan's more and more. Sometimes Nathan would have a whore or two there. And he'd always ask Mark if he wanted to. Big women, little women. Hispanic, white, black. No, thanks, Mark would say. Even though he wasn't getting any at home. But he just wanted Maddy, or so he thought. He was heartbroken.

14

He came in and saw his wife standing at the sink in the kitchen, her back toward him. And as if seeing her for the first time in weeks, he noticed that her shoulder blades protruded almost grotesquely. Of course, he just saw her this morning and the morning before and the morning before and on and on and he wondered why he did not notice her shoulders until this moment.

The door closed behind him and she did not turn around to say hello. He remembered a time when she would run from whatever it was that she was doing and kiss him wetly. Squeal for joy. Say, I missed you, Mark, and bury her face in his neck. Stick her hand down his pants and get on her knees. Of course, those emotions never last. But aren't they supposed to be taken over by a deeper, more mature kind of love? Where was that?

He decided to say hello and be affectionate. It was a

conscious, deliberate decision. It was not how he normally greeted her anymore. Something in the angles of her shoulder blades prompted it. It was not his normal way of approaching her when he came home. He walked toward her, approaching her boney back and slipped his hands around her waist. She turned her head around and looked at him with a grim curiosity. He had wanted her to turn around and kiss him or smile sweetly and the suspicious glance she gave him, the raised eyebrow, disheartened him. He slowly unwrapped his hands and sighed loudly. He pulled a beer from the fridge and went into the living room and watched TV.

What's wrong with you, she said, standing in the doorway to the living room with her arms crossed.

I just tried to be nice and you didn't care.

This is my only night off work this week. I've been working too hard.

Is that an apology?

I guess so.

Will you bring me another beer?

Yeah.

She came back with two beers and sat next to him on the couch.

You look really thin.

I've lost some weight.

Every time I set foot in this house you're in the kitchen cooking.

She smiled widely at him—a strange grin, one he found

unsettling. I like to cook, she said. She filled up a bowl with pot and smoked. Mark smoked. They stared at the TV.

Madeleine went into the bathroom and shut the door. He heard the water run in the tub. He walked quietly up to the door and ever so softly, leaned his head against it. He heard her pee. He heard her brush her teeth. He heard the mirror cabinet open. He thought he could hear her clothes drop to the floor, the wisp of cloth against tile. She shut the water off in the tub and Mark tensed against the door, fearing she could hear him listening in on her. He slid down and crouched.

He heard her toe break the water and she said oh and then made a hissing noise. Then she said ah aha. Her body dropped in, bit by bit and she moaned when she was all the way in. The water sloshed. Was he imagining he could feel the steam come out of the crack at the bottom of the door? He put his hand out to see if he really could. It felt warm and damp. He put his hand to his face and it felt wet.

He heard her move around, heard the water moving around. He heard her breathe deeply, exhaling loudly. He stood up and decided to knock.

Hey, Maddy, can I come in?

What for?

Brush my teeth. Take a piss.

The door's locked.

Why the fuck is the door locked, he said and turned the knob and indeed, the door was locked. What the fuck is your problem, he said. I've got to take a piss.

He heard her get up out of the tub, the water making a sucking noise and seconds later she stood there, a large pink towel
wrapped around her dripping body. Her face was bright red and
her hair lay in wet strands around her face.

Come in.

Why'd you lock the door?

I wanted to take a long, peaceful bath and not be disturbed.
That's it, she said. She dropped the towel and stepped gingerly
back in the tub and Mark noticed her skinniness acutely now.
Her hipbones jutted out. Her chest bone was pronounced. Her
breasts lay against her body like pancakes. With one forceful
move, she pulled the shower curtain shut.

Mark sat down on the toilet and said, baby, you look really
skinny.

Maddy sighed but said nothing.

Can I open the shower curtain? he asked.

She put her head outside of the curtain. One hand grasped
the pink plastic material and she was angry now and he could
tell by her jaw hanging stiffly. I just want to take a goddamn
bath in peace, she said, something I like to do. Something I do
with regularity and you aren't letting me.

Maddy, pull the curtain and let me look at you.

She yanked the curtain open, the water sloshing forward and
then she sat back heavily, her arms covering her breasts. A light
film of bubbles covered the surface of the faintly blue water. It
smelled of jasmine. Her mouth was open, her face covered with
sweat and she said, here I am. Now you can look at me.

What's wrong, baby. Why aren't you eating?

Mark pulled his T-shirt over his head and dropped it to the ground. He was sweating.

I'm going to have to pick up that T-shirt you know.

Well what should I do with it?

You should put it in the hamper. That's where I'm going to put it later.

It's not dirty.

Then I'll have to put it in your drawer, instead.

Madeleine abruptly dropped her head under the water. When she came back up her cheeks were swollen and she spit out a stream of water like a fountain.

That was lovely. The bubbles must taste nice, he said.

Again she went under, quickly, again her cheeks ballooned out, but this time she spit the water at Mark, hitting him on his hairless chest.

Thank you, he said.

Anytime, she replied. She closed her eyes and let her tongue drop out to her chin.

Mark slid off the toilet seat and sat pressed against the sweating tub. His hair was wet now, his face dripping like hers. He put a hand in the water. He wanted to touch his wife, who seemed to be disappearing. He wanted to get in the tub with her. The water scorched his hand.

Jesus, Maddy, this water is hot as hell.

I like it that way.

Can I come in with you?

Oh, Mark.

Please? It'll be fun. We haven't taken a bath together in a long time.

We haven't for a reason.

Let me come in. You could show me one of your tricks. You never do your tricks for me anymore. You used to do them extra well in the tub.

Neither of us does tricks for the other. Neither of us does anything for the other anymore.

Don't say that. That's not true. Let me come in.

Maddy looked away and Mark decided that this was a yes. He took off his pants and tried dipping a toe into the water.

This is impossible. You have to let me run some cold water.

Absolutely not, she said, and ran her hands over her bright face.

He put a foot in. It burned. Slowly, painfully, he managed to squeeze into the tub with her. His legs pressed against the sides and hers lay in between his, their backs against each end of the tub. The water rose to the edge and began draining through the hole underneath the spout.

Jesus, this water is so hot I can't breathe.

Then get out.

Mark stared at his wife.

Maddy, stop being such a bitch. We have to stop being this way to each other, he said, and grabbed her calf.

Let go of my leg.

No.

Get out of my bath.

No.

He grabbed her other calf.

You're a bastard.

You're a fucking bitch.

Maddy stood up and he tried to pull her back down, still holding onto her legs. She slipped and steadied herself by holding onto his shoulders and he let go of her legs and held her wrists there, held her against his shoulders.

You're going to kill me, she said.

She sat down again, shaken, plopping down directly on his lap.

I almost cracked my head open in my own bathtub and this is my only day off and you've ruined it.

I'm sorry.

You are not.

When was the last time we fucked, Maddy?

They sat together now, uncomfortably, their arms around each other.

I don't know, Mark. I don't know.

15

Mark tried. He tried talking to her, he tried touching her, he tried doing things for her like buying flowers that would sit hopelessly in a vase on the kitchen table. She wouldn't even notice them. He tried kissing her, smiling at her, watching TV with her. He tried to take her out for dinner, but she wouldn't let him, no way, she said, I don't want to spend money at some stupid restaurant. I'll pay, he'd say, and she just shook her head, no. You used to like going out to restaurants. Leave me alone, she'd say. She was so thin he was frightened of her.

Miraculously, she stopped cooking for him all the time. At first he was relieved; her behavior had been so fierce. Then she stopped cooking altogether. He'd make himself a sandwich and ask her if she wanted anything and she'd say no. He knew she hadn't been eating much for a long time. But now she didn't even try to hide the fact that she didn't eat at all.

If she wasn't working then she'd watch TV, her eyes glazed from hunger, her hair brittle around her head, deep blue bags under her eyes. Who was this? He bought her chocolates, he bought her lingerie that would never fit her anymore, he rented her favorite movies. Thick tongued, haggard, half dead, she'd ignore everything, sitting on the couch, a tense corpse, coughing hollowly, chain-smoking cigarettes. The thinner she got the more power she had over him. The smaller she was the more he feared her.

The smell of her changed, the shape of her changed and her face, her energy her everything became more extreme, more out of control. He cared about her still but he had to give up and he knew he did the right thing. For him, anyway. No, for both of them. They had nothing anymore but fear and avoidance. He thought sometimes, drunk, driving home from Nathan's, a useless half-mast hard-on in his pants from a porn movie, that she

had given up something, everything—not just her hardness—
her everything the minute he kissed her in his car and it just
took him this long to figure it out.

He ran because he was scared because he couldn't stand her
anymore. He walked through the mall where he worked and
a petite, dark-haired woman walked by. She wore a nice dress
that came down to her ankles and small gold earrings and he
knew who she was. She worked in the clothing store next to the
computer store where he worked. He saw her almost every day
after that. Getting an Orange Julius and a hot dog her thin little
feet in flat navy shoes making a wisp-wisp noise as she shimmied
back to the store. He looked at her really closely, really looked.
She knew he was looking at her and she remained composed. She
was cool, never blushing, never fidgeting. He imagined her
breasts. Round and small, beneath his hands. Fleshy breasts, the
skin moist and bouncy. Not deflated, not dry, not flat and sad.
He imagined the girl's pussy tasting like wet, fresh cut grass.
How could he not think of these things?

He knew something true and solid about this girl. This
woman who worked at the clothing store, a respectable store, a
nice place, would struggle with him always. Would push against
his hands with her knees, just enough to make him harder, as
he spread her legs apart. She'd protest and her breath would
quicken. Her muscles tense. And although he is not a big man,
far from it, he is bigger than her and he would feel that way, feel
himself truly overpower her. She would never beg for it. She
would never give in completely.

He watched this girl for a while. No boy picked her up after work ever. She walked to her dainty Japanese car, a black purse hanging from her slim shoulder, car keys in her hand, and drove off steadily, her seatbelt fastened and the radio turned on at medium volume. She was not taken. But it wasn't her that was made for him. Someone like her. He'll leave here, go out West. He'll start over and get away from it all. And that's when he'll find her.

16

What's wrong with me?

Nothing's wrong with you.

How come you don't want to be with me anymore?

It's not that I don't want to be with you.

What is it then?

Jesus, Madeleine.

What? What is it. You have to tell me. You have to. You owe me that much.

I don't know.

Look at me.

I am looking at you.

You look away when you talk.

It just isn't working out.

Why not? What's wrong? What don't you like about me?

It's not that I don't like you.

Why do you want to give up?

Madeleine . . .

I grow my hair because you want me to. I don't wear red lipstick because you don't want me to.

It's not those things.

I am so dedicated to you.

I can't handle it.

Handle what?

Handle you.

What's that supposed to mean?

You're sick.

You've made me that way. You don't give me enough. Of course I'm sick. You don't call. You're always out with Nathan.

See. You're not happy either. We don't make each other happy.

You don't try.

I *do* try.

Try harder.

I tried as hard as I can.

That's a fucking lie.

No it's not.

Bullshit. If you cared you'd make this work. If you gave a shit about me, you'd try harder.

I do care about you.

How? How do you care about me? What do you do to care about me?

I love you, Maddy.

It can't just be a feeling in your head, Mark. You have to act. You have to show me.

I've tried Maddy and it hasn't worked. We deserve better than this. We deserve to be happy.

Why can't we be happy together?

I don't know. You're never happy with me. I'm always doing something wrong. I'm tired of being the bad guy.

Then treat me better.

I did the best I could, it didn't work.

Fuck you. Fuck you. You're a piece of shit.

Don't cry, Maddy.

Fuck you. You're giving up on me.

Don't cry.

You're sick of me, that's it.

I'm not sick of you. I'm tired of failing you.

You're sick of fucking me.

No.

Yes you are.

I still love being inside of you.

Not enough to make this work.

I can't handle this.

Fuck me.

No, Maddy. That's not the answer to our problems.

You can't fuck me, can you?

We can't be together just for that.

You can't get it up for me. You're sick of my pussy.

Stop it Maddy. Jesus Christ, I won't put up with this. You wonder why I'm leaving you.

What?

You fucking wonder why we're not working out. You're so fucking hostile. That's what's wrong with you. You are so angry and so sick.

I'm upset, Mark. I'm sorry. I'm just upset. Please, please. I'll be easier on you. I'm sorry. Don't be mad at me.

I'm not mad at you. I just can't do this anymore.

Please Mark. I'm hurting. I'm not always like this.

I can't handle it anymore.

I'm upset. Deal with it. You can't handle anything. That's the whole problem. You just run away when things get rough.

It's not that simple.

It's not that complicated either, Mark. Either you're in it or you're not. Either you make it work or you don't.

I tried, Maddy. I tried as much as I can and I can't give you what you need.

I cooked dinner all the time. I bought your favorite beer.

Stop it.

Why after all this time are you leaving me? Why? I'll be better. You're killing me.

Listen I'm sorry. Nothing's wrong with you. We don't belong together.

Goddamn you. You think I can't take the truth.

You want the truth?

Yeah.

You're too weak. And you're killing yourself.

I'm weak? Because I love you and want to make this work, I'm weak?

Not because of that.

Why then? Why am I weak?

I don't know. You just are. Jesus, I can't talk about this anymore.

Look at me. Look at me. You call me weak and you can't even look at me when you say it. Fucking pussy.

I'm moving out tomorrow. I'll pay half the rent until you find a cheaper place.

Fuck you. I don't need your help.

I'm sorry Maddy.

Don't apologize to me. I don't want your pity.

I love you.

Fuck you. Get out of my house. Get out now. Get out of here.

17

She ran and ran until there was nowhere to go. Through the fridge, through her childhood, through her adolescence, lickety-split, running through the cookbooks, up and down the alley behind their house, round and round the block with her mother, swinging the jump rope over her head again and again, her feet moving, skipping. One two three. One two three. Put it here Mark, put it here, make me come again and again, I'll show you, look at me, my fist in me, my arm in me, fuck me again and again and then what? Good God she's tired and scared and where to next? Stuck in this hospital, in an anorexic ward, some asshole lady shrink wanting to talk about self esteem and image and draw a picture of yourself how you imagine yourself, what does she think, that I'm some stupid kid and playing with crayons will make me feel better. Maddy draws a picture of a starlet-type girl, voluptuous, but not fat, with sunglasses and lipstick. Is this how you see yourself, the shrink asks, looking at Maddy with eyes so widely open it looks like it hurts, looking at her so sincerely, leaning forward in her chair, what do you think about this picture, Madeleine. I think I want big tits again, you moron cunt, Maddy thinks, all the while smiling and saying, I don't know, that's how I used to look I guess.

Big floppy breasts, big fleshy thighs he grabbed onto, round rolling stomach he kissed and bit and now what does she have to give him or anyone? Running to work, her uniform so clean and straight, not one stain, how can that be, after work, leaning over the sink at midnight in the bathroom, scrubbing out the spots of ketchup and gravy with a laundry brush and detergent, her back hurting, but do it now, she thinks rather than put it off until later. Slipping into bed with him so quietly, he doesn't wake, getting up an hour before him in the morning and showering, wash hair then body, then face, then shave legs and then off to work the breakfast shift for Jane. Get there half an hour early and drink three cups of coffee and smoke three cigarettes while organizing the waitress station, clean ketchup bottles, no gook around the edges, fill salt and pepper shakers, wipe down all the menus, clean the coffee machines with a wire scrub brush, and then what? Then what? Work lunch and dinner shifts if possible, which it almost always is because so many lazy shits who don't care if their bills are late, who don't care if their phone gets shut off for a few days.

Men she waits on looking at her like she's not much of anything, not the way they used to look at her and it's not because she's waitressing, she knows, no, it's because she looks like shit. No more of that. I want my tits back, you stupid moron cunt shrink, she thinks. I'll get them back, they haven't gone away forever. The shrink says, Maddy, are you listening to me? You look very far off. Maddy? Where are you? What are you thinking about? Do you like it when your mother visits you here, or does it upset you?

When my mother visits. Maddy thinks, bringing her Tupperware sweating with lukewarm food, sitting in the common room, nervous and watching the clock because she always visits for one hour, no more no less, miserable and talking about things Maddy couldn't care less about, her sister, her cousins, a new item of furniture in the house. Do I like it when she visits, Maddy says, I don't know. I don't feel one way or the other about her visits. I can tell you though, she says to the shrink, *she* doesn't like it. But who would. This place is pretty depressing. You probably don't like it. But they pay you to be here. The shrink says, I didn't ask whether your mom or I liked visiting with you, I asked if you liked it when your mom visits. There is an edge of impatience in the shrink's voice and Maddy thinks, poor cow eyes, she hates her job. Understandably.

Do you want to let your husband come and visit the shrink asks, because Maddy, after passing out cold at work, her boss unable to arouse her, while being carried away by paramedics with an oxygen mask over her face, pulled the mask off herself as soon as she was conscious and said, do not let my husband visit me. Okay? You hear me, and the paramedic put the oxygen mask back on her and said okay, okay, just breathe, that's it, just breathe. No, she says to Dr. Barrabo, I absolutely do not want him here. It might be a good idea, says the shrink.

I'm too tired, she thinks, I'm tired and I can't stop moving and I don't know where to go, but she doesn't say that to the big-eyed, tilted-head bitch in front of her. She says, I just need to get away from here, start over somewhere else, I'm fine, Dr. Barrabo, I *want* to gain weight, I do. I believe you, Maddy, says the shrink, but there are still things we should talk about. And I don't think running away is the answer. Fine Maddy thinks, just fine for you, you stay here in the stinking awful loser town, I've got better places to go, but she says, I don't want to run away, I just want to have a fresh start, that's all. The shrink looks so serious, so cow-eyed, Maddy shivers she wants to hit her so badly, change that awful expression on her long all-eyeball face. Dr. Barrrabo says, I think moving could be a good thing, but first you should stay here and resolve some issues, so you don't take it all with you.

Take it all? Resolve some issues? Maddy thinks, how do you resolve your life, dissolve your life, don't take it with you? Leave it behind? Wrap it up in a nice package, put a bow on it? Why not take it with me, it's my life, I own it. But she says, I feel resolved about things. Really I do, all the while thinking, yes sir shrinky dink, thinking God is our forty five minutes up yet and then it is and Maddy's alone again and she hears her neighbors cough and she gets up and walks around a bit, towing her IV alongside herself. Smiling at this nurse, hello to that nurse, goes into the common room and watches TV for four hours straight, takes her meal in there because she can, because she's such a well behaved patient, they all love her. Time for weigh in, standing in line with the other girls, pussies, she thinks, pussies all of them, except maybe that one, the really really skinny one, the one with dark hair on her face, bald patches on her head, smells bad even though you have to shower here everyday, looks like death. Maddy smiles at her on the way back from another happy weigh-in, good job Maddy, one and a half pounds today, the girl stares back without blinking, her bottom jaw sticking out in an very unattractive way.

The girl's name is Nancy, some crazed teenager, only sixteen, looks like she's forty going on a hundred. Maddy hears the nurses talking about Nancy, voices low, pissed-off sounding, words used to describe her are hopeless and disgusting and sad. Maddy walks by her bed and smiles at her again and again, finally, out of control, foam on the edges of her mouth, Nancy says, what the fuck are you looking at? and Maddy just laughs. Late at night Maddy walks up to her bed and she's awake, Maddy knows it, even though she's laying there stiff as a board not moving, Maddy walks straight up to the bed and looks at this girl, this girl with two deep sockets for eyes this girl who stinks of rot, and says, want to go smoke a cigarette? Nancy gets up without saying anything and they both go into the common room, the night nurse hasn't found them yet, she's still in her little lit-up box of a station at the end of the hall, the two girls go in there and Maddy produces two stale Marlboros and a pack of matches and they both sit down on a couch, right next to each other. Maddy strikes a match and lights Nancy's first, the girl says nothing, Maddy says you're welcome, the girl says nothing but smiles, or kind of smiles, her teeth as green as moss, her mouth open and that's where the smell is coming from the strongest, Maddy thinks, from inside her, coming out her holes, her mouth, her ears for god's sake. The two girls sit there and look at each other and look away, comfortable either way, sitting very close, and smoke.